THE NIGHTMARE BEGINS

Kinsolving would not have recognized the creature that burst from the mansion doors. Fiery red eyes blazed as the beast rushed across the lawn toward them. Fingers hooked like talons raked the air. Worst of all was the demented shrieking.

It was obvious that they were the rampaging Trekan's target...

Other Avon Books by
Robert E. Vardeman

THE MASTERS OF SPACE SERIES

(#1) THE STELLAR DEATH PLAN
(#2) THE ALIEN WEB

Avon Books are available at special quantity discounts for bulk purchases for sales promotions, premiums, fund raising or educational use. Special books, or book excerpts, can also be created to fit specific needs.

For details write or telephone the office of the Director of Special Markets, Avon Books, Dept. FP, 105 Madison Avenue, New York, New York 10016, 212-481-5653.

A PLAGUE IN PARADISE

ROBERT E. VARDEMAN

AVON
PUBLISHERS OF BARD, CAMELOT, DISCUS AND FLARE BOOKS

MASTERS OF SPACE #3: A PLAGUE IN PARADISE is an original publication of Avon Books. This work has never before appeared in book form. This work is a novel. Any similarity to actual persons or events is purely coincidental.

AVON BOOKS
A division of
The Hearst Corporation
105 Madison Avenue
New York, New York 10016

Copyright © 1987 by Robert E. Vardeman
Published by arrangement with the author
Library of Congress Catalog Card Number: 87-91158
ISBN: 0-380-75006-6

All rights reserved, which includes the right to reproduce this book or portions thereof in any form whatsoever except as provided by the U.S. Copyright Law. For information address Howard Morhaim Literary Agency, 501 Fifth Avenue, New York, New York 10017.

First Avon Printing: September 1987

AVON TRADEMARK REG. U.S. PAT. OFF. AND IN OTHER COUNTRIES, MARCA REGISTRADA, HECHO EN U.S.A.

Printed in the U.S.A.

K-R 10 9 8 7 6 5 4 3 2 1

For Gwynne Scholz,
the naked DEA agent
falling through the ceiling,
the $13,000 kidney, being fed to alligators,
and all the other great stories

CHAPTER ONE

"IT'S NOT POSSIBLE," Barton Kinsolving muttered to himself as he struggled with the luxury yacht's simple, foolproof controls. "The Lorr police vessel is homing in on us."

"They're following us?" Lark Versalles brushed back long strands of her fine blond hair and revealed her forehead. The glamour dyes she had injected subcutaneously whirled about in complex eddies just above her eyebrows and slowly turned different shades of purple. Kinsolving tried to decide if this color change meant the woman was agitated or if she felt only annoyance at the delay in leaving the system.

For Kinsolving, having the alien spacecraft homing in on them meant more than simple irritation at being detained. He had escaped the planet of Zeta Orgo 4 and its arachnoid inhabitants only minutes ahead of the Lorr police. It mattered little to the spiderlike creatures that he had thwarted a plan—the Stellar Death Plan—of his former employers that would have destroyed the aliens' minds. In their oddly twisted way of looking at the world, the arachnoids had not betrayed a benefactor by turning him over to the Lorr.

Kinsolving stared at the vidscreen and the dim image of the approaching Lorr spaceship. When he had worked for Interstellar Materials on the planet Deepdig as a mining supervisor, he had been wrongly implicated in the death of a Lorr agent-captain. The trial and conviction had been swift, and alien justice required exile to a prison world.

He had escaped—the only sentient being to do so. And Barton Kinsolving had become the preoccupation of every Lorr peace officer.

Even worse, those in power at IM eagerly sought him, too. They wanted nothing less than the total extinction of hundreds of alien races populating known space. Genocide. Even thinking of their hideous scheme on Zeta Orgo 4 made him shudder. He had stopped them this time. He had seen one of the IM directors killed and, for all he knew, the assassin Cameron had died, also. Kinsolving shuddered. He dared not take the killer's death as a fact. Cameron had proven himself too wily in the past to succumb to an ambush while guarded by his specially designed robots.

"They're getting closer," Lark said. The purples swirling beneath her skin faded and became light yellows, giving her a jaundiced, diseased look. Kinsolving had to interpret this as increasing dread on her part. He felt as ill as she looked.

"I'm doing all I can. The overrides on the ship make it hard to work." Not for the first time, he cursed the safety features that prevented casual access to the controls. Its former owner, Rani duLong, might have been able to get around the safeties but she had been murdered by Cameron's infernal robot killers. Kinsolving and Lark had escaped only through good luck and a small bit of skill on his part in fixing the ship's hyperspace shift engine electronics.

Kinsolving dived under the control panel and found the spots where he had shorted out the safeties once before. Small charred areas marked his successes. What might fail because of his efforts he dared not think about.

"Lark," he called out from under the panel, "what's the course indicator reading?"

"Something about, oh, it's set for Paradise!"

"I don't care where we jump as long as we do it soon. Is that the lowest numbered reading?" He had no time for complex alignment. The first star system that matched in the navigation computer would be their destination.

"Yes."

He thrust his hand upward, putting his thumb on one exposed contact and his thick index finger on another. Kinsolving screamed as pain assailed him—but the pain came not from the minute electrical current finding a least resistance path through his sweat-dampened skin but from the impact of the hyperspacial shift.

He felt as if he were falling down an infinite well. Colors more vivid than any in Lark's cosmetic arsenal spun in demented kaleidoscope patterns before—behind—his eyes, through his brain, deep into his very soul. And the sounds! He always heard phantom music, haunting, alluring. He tried to turn to face its source, but it changed as he moved. Always, it came from a different direction, a place beyond sight and hearing. Kinsolving struggled to make out the eerie tune, to put a name on it, to be able to remember it.

As always, he failed. The churning in his gut subsided. The music drifted away. The wild vortices of color collapsed and normal sight returned. With it came the light pseudogravity of shift space and an odd stench.

It took Kinsolving several seconds to realize that the skin on his fingers had burned. He jerked back, breaking the contact.

"Bart, darling, what happened?" asked Lark. Her voice carried the plaintive quality which demanded that he respond and make everything right again in her spoiled, rich universe.

"I probably ruined the control circuits." He sucked on his burned fingers to cut off the oxygen to the wounds. Crawling from under the panel, he looked up at the woman and, not for the first time, felt a surge of emotion. Putting a definition on what that emotion really was proved even more difficult than identifying the phantom music of pipes and synthesizers created during shift.

Love? He doubted it. Lark had inadvertently rescued him from the Lorr prison world. For that he owed her much. No one else had ever escaped that cruel exile. But what he felt for her transcended simple duty. He had assumed an obligation when he had allowed her to accompany him. For her, he provided a new and exciting diversion. Kinsolving wondered if Lark understood how truly dangerous it was being near him. Possibly. She was not a stupid woman.

Duty and gratitude, yes, and more: these he felt for her. And friendship. He liked her in spite of the differences in their backgrounds and outlooks. She had seen the horror Interstellar Materials sought to create by their genocidal Plan and had aided him. Deep down, though, she did not feel the commitment he did, the outrage, the stark revulsion at Cameron and IM's Chairman Fremont.

Lark Versalles skimmed through life, sampling daintily, tasting the sweet wines and never finding the bitter.

"The ship's going to need a long time in dock to fix," he said.

"Don't worry about it. My credit's still good. Especially on Paradise!"

"What is this world?" he asked, pulling himself up and buckling himself down in the pilot's acceleration couch. He only half listened to her gushing explanation as he scanned the limited controls. Most were nothing more than warning lights. The ship's on-board robot repair crew toiled to fix most minor problems. The major ones he had created required human attention and the complete equipment of an orbiting dry dock.

A quick glance at the vidscreen showed only the jumbled patterns of hyperspace. The Lorr had tracked them too quickly back in the Zeta Orgo 4 system. Something—someone—had alerted them to his presence. They had no reason to suspect this luxury yacht of harboring their prime fugitive from justice.

By choosing a world at random, Kinsolving knew he had eluded the Lorr—unless their technology far exceeded that of the humans. Could the aliens follow a starship through a shift and pinpoint its destination? Kinsolving shuddered again, a mental picture forming of them coming out of hyperspace and finding the Lorr police vessel waiting.

"... spent months there. It's photonic, Bart, darling. *Anything* you want, and I mean *anything!*"

"Paradise?"

Lark swung about and snuggled close, her long arms circling his neck. Her face blocked out the vidscreen and control panel. It wasn't a displeasing situation, but Kinsolving experienced a pang of uneasiness at being unable to watch the control panel telltales. Too many circuits aboard ship had been destroyed to grow careless.

Lark's bright blue eyes bored into his dark ones. Her lips parted slightly, sending waves of light greens radiating from her mouth in a delicate spiderweb. The woman's cheeks flushed a bright pink, then turned a more passionate red.

"We're free of them. The Lorr, IM, all of them. Let's relax and enjoy ourselves, Barton, my dearest."

She bent forward and kissed him. Kinsolving resisted slightly, thinking he saw a flashing red light on the control panel. He took a quick look and saw nothing. He had seen Lark's cheeks blazing crimson as her desire mounted. He reached out and put his strong arms around her, drew her closer. There might be better ways of passing the time in the infinite expanse of hyperspace, but Barton Kinsolving could not think what they might be. Not with a woman like Lark so close.

"Again, Bart, please," begged Lark. She knelt behind the couch and put her arms around his neck. Her soft blond hair brushed the side of his face, the sunlight-gold strands floating up in the breeze to tickle his nose. He brushed them away and reached out to press the appropriate controls on the panel.

"Time to shift back to normal space," he said.

She brightened at the idea of again being on Paradise. She swung about and dropped into the acceleration couch beside him, her hand firmly clutching his bulkier one.

Kinsolving gulped as the starship dropped from hyperspace, the full array of sensory confusion assaulting him. He strained to hear the phantom music, but heard nothing this time. In its place, he tasted metallic bitterness on the sides of his tongue, and his feet froze as if he had thrust them into a bucket of icy water. Keeping him from complaining at the shift was the firm grip Lark kept on him the entire time. Knowing that someone shared all this with him eased the burden.

The vidscreen lit up with a display of approach numbers from the Paradise Port Authority and a small picture of the planet's surface. Kinsolving frowned. Such views normally came through the on-board cameras. They were still almost fifty AUs away, a distance making such detail impossible.

"They transmit a picture of what we're going to see," Lark supplied. "Isn't it wonderful!"

"Wonderful," Kinsolving agreed halfheartedly. He didn't like the idea of the Port Authority taking control of the vidscreen. The Lorr starship might be only seconds behind and he would be unable to detect it. Another shift might be necessary; he had to know if the aliens had followed. That new shift, if required, might destroy them. He would prefer to let the Paradise dry docks refit the yacht. Too many amber and red indicator lights popped up, showing how he had abused the vessel.

He toggled the ship-to-station communicator. "Earth ship *von Neumann* desiring repair facilities."

"Attention, *von Neumann*," came the instant response. "We are sunward less than point one AU and read your problems. Are you able to reach Paradise orbit unassisted?"

Kinsolving poked at the vidscreen controls. The Paradise Port Authority had not released the vidscreen to allow him to pick up the other ship.

"We can attain orbit unassisted. Can you release remote override on my vidscreen?"

A tiny pop of static and a man so handsome that Kinsolving had to consider him beautiful appeared on the vidscreen. "Captain Luxor of the Paradise Assistance Fleet," he said by way of introduction. "Most of the ships coming to our planet like the view of the surface. I understand your problem, however."

"Oh, we're going to land on Paradise," cut in Lark. "I've enjoyed my other stays here."

"But we do have some on-board problems," Kinsolving finished.

"Do you have a Pleasure Code?" asked the captain of the other ship.

"It's the same as for Galaxy Pharmaceuticals and Medical Techtronics—GPMT."

Kinsolving stared at Lark. Was she lying? Then he realized that he knew little about her background. She never spoke of her family, of former lovers, of friends. Always Lark Versalles lived for the instant. Let it pass and it was as if she forgot.

"Lark Versalles," came Captain Luxor's reply, "welcome back to Paradise. We will happily escort you to Almost Paradise."

"Almost Paradise?" Kinsolving asked the woman.

"Their orbiting station. Paradise caters to all races. Almost Paradise allows time for quarantine, if necessary, acclimation, a chance to anticipate all that can come true on the surface."

"If they can repair the ship." Kinsolving went cold inside when Captain Luxor's image flickered on the screen, then firmed again. The captain had cut for transmission, probably to the main data banks on Paradise, and had not wanted Kinsolving to know.

"You are aboard a ship licensed to the sister of Aron duLong, chairman of Terra Computronics. Is Rani aboard?"

"She's just loaned us the ship," Kinsolving said quickly, turning even colder inside. Her body still rode in the main storage hold of the *von Neumann*, secure in a vacuum coffin.

Kinsolving did not want to consider a murder charge placed against him on yet another world.

"GPMT credit will suffice," said the captain. With those words, Kinsolving got a clearer picture of Paradise. If someone could pay, any trouble could be smoothed over.

"Should I dock or will you send out a grapple tug?" he asked of Luxor.

"We have already fastened lines to your hull plates."

Kinsolving tried to verify but found the sensors on the composite hull to be malfunctioning, like so much aboard the yacht. He had not heard or felt the vibrations from the magnetic grapples being attached to the special tug plates, but his Doppler radar showed a closing vector on Almost Paradise impossible without the lines.

The ship docked gently, barely jarring them. Lark shot out of her couch, her face radiant with every color of the rainbow. Not even trying to hide her excitement, Lark pulled on his arm and said, "Hurry, Bart, darling. There's *so* much to do aboard Almost Paradise. If it wasn't so much fun on-planet, I'd spend all my time on the station."

Kinsolving followed reluctantly. His bleak mood contrasted sharply with Lark's ebullience. So much needed to be done and he had no clear idea how to accomplish it. Cameron had killed the Lorr agent-captain; how could Kinsolving clear himself? IM had been prevented from burning out the brains of the aliens on Zeta Orgo; did they pursue their mad scheme on other worlds? Probably. He needed to find out for certain. The aliens might not know of the danger posed by Interstellar Materials. They might even deny any human capable of such intricate planning, but Kinsolving knew. And he had to prevent Fremont and the others from mass killing, whether the aliens appreciated his sacrifices or not.

The airlock cycled open. To his surprise, Kinsolving's ears did not pop from poor pressure-matching between ship and station. Someone had taken the trouble to mesh perfectly. A cool, scented breeze blew inward and peaceful pale green lights shone on a tastefully decorated reception area.

"Welcome, Lark," greeted a petite woman, hands held out for Lark to grip. They kissed chastely. Something about the small woman's attitude told Kinsolving that, for all the overt friendliness, she was only an employee. Her smile came too quickly. Every detail about her neat, conservative dress spoke of carefully chosen effect. Kinsolving held back asking her what she would have worn had she been given a chance to choose her own clothing. He guessed that her tastes paralleled Lark's. Something flashy, something skimpy, something scandalous.

But to dress like that in Lark's presence would have put the woman in competition. Kinsolving had to wonder how the greeting would have differed if he had arrived without Lark.

"Welcome to you, too, sir," the woman said, her small hand cool against his. She shook hands firmly, quickly, then backed away without making eye contact. Her every action was one of deference.

"Please accept my personal apologies about accommodations aboard Almost Paradise. We cannot put you into the Royal Suite because of a special conference on-planet."

"Conference?" Kinsolving asked.

"Terra Recreations operates Paradise as a restful environment where any pleasure is available," she said, more robotic than human as she slipped into her sales speech. "From time to time we allow alien races the use of our facilities for interspecies diplomatic conferences. Currently, we are honored with seven different species on-planet while they conduct business with Earth representatives on trade and other matters of mutual interest."

"But the Royal Suite." Lark pouted. "I had my heart set on staying there again."

"Oh, Lark," the small woman said, sounding genuinely sorry, "we just can't. The Trekan ambassador requires time to acclimate himself to Paradise's atmosphere. The Royal Suite is the only one suitable for complex gas exchange."

"It doesn't matter," said Kinsolving. "We're not going to demand anything that lavish." He glared at Lark when she started to protest his peasant attitudes.

"I'm so glad you understand, sir," said the woman. For the first time, her pale gray eyes locked with his dark ones. Kinsolving tried to read some message in that gaze and failed. He felt, however, that he had been thoroughly examined and found wanting.

"You do have *something* suitable, don't you?" asked Lark. "We've been cooped up in the ship for ever so long."

"Will the Xanadu Suite be adequate for your needs?" the woman asked. From the color shifts in Lark's cosmetic dyes, Kinsolving saw that the answer was a resounding yes.

"We'll need repairs done on the ship," said Kinsolving. "We have special cargo, though, and I'd appreciate it if the workmen didn't disturb anything in the hold."

"Sir, our workers, both robotic and human, are always discreet." She made it sound as if Kinsolving had mortally insulted her.

"Good." He did not trust himself to say anything more. This wasn't his world. Lark Versalles fit in perfectly and he stood out like a nova in the night. Kinsolving trailed along as the two women went down a long, curving corridor leading to the Xanadu Suite.

They entered an immense, lavishly furnished lounge area that seemed all the larger because it was deserted. A small noise alerted Kinsolving. He turned to his right in time to see a man duck from sight behind a long, imported Earth oakwood bar. Kinsolving started to go after the man but Lark called for him.

He looked back and failed to catch sight of the man again. Kinsolving tried to shrug it off. Another servant, perhaps. But the brief glimpse Kinsolving had got belied that.

Barton Kinsolving caught up with Lark and their servant-guide, even more uneasy than he had been before.

CHAPTER TWO

CAMERON'S PALE GRAY EYES flickered open and light painfully assaulted his optic nerves. The man lay still, not moving a muscle—unable to move. Panic welled up within him but Cameron fought it down. There had to be an explanation for his paralysis, for the light in his face, for the odd odors causing his nostrils to flare.

Smell—antiseptics. Light—disinfectant UV. Paralysis. —life-coma.

Memory flooded back now as the ocean of drugs in his body began to ebb. He had been injured on Zeta Orgo 4.

Damn Kinsolving!

A voice farther away than infinity said, "Response. The reading went off-scale."

"Must be a residual thought rising," said another voice.

Cameron concentrated. And remembered. He had been in the Interstellar Materials warehouse on ZOo and had laid a trap for the meddling former mining supervisor. Kinsolving had walked directly into the trap. But he had turned the brain burner against Cameron's robot. Short circuits. Power surges. Spikes strong enough to fry delicate artificial intelligence circuits. Cameron remembered the sight of his robots gyrating wildly and exploding. Some had crashed into walls while others had simply ceased functioning.

His heart pumped firmly now. Blood rushed through sleeping arteries. Oxygen burned in his lungs and he tried to cough, to choke, to breathe, to steal back life from the induced coma.

"More response. He's a strong one, coming out of the life-coma this fast."

"Son of a bitch hates harder than anyone I ever knew. That's what's bringing him around. Bet on it."

"You'd just be throwing your money down a black hole.

I know him. I had to repair him after his lab caught fire a couple years ago."

Cameron listened to the idle chatter. Memory returned fully now. He knew the two doctors who worked to pull him through from the other side of death. The life-coma had been necessary to return him to Gamma Tertius 4. The medical facilities on the arachnoids' planet had been unable to give him the treatment required to insure full recovery.

Cameron's lip twitched into a sneer. What did the damned Bizarres know of medicine, anyway? The Bizzies could never heal a human. Such art lay far beyond their abilities. He was better off back on GT4 in the hands—real hands!—of human and human-designed robotic doctors.

"Full response. He ought to be out of the life-coma now," came the disembodied voice, no longer distant.

"I am out of it, fool," Cameron protested. His voice came out as a weak mewling.

"He's vectored home to us," said the other, with some satisfaction. "Nothing more to do now but wait." Cameron felt a hand on his shoulder that was supposed to reassure him. "You'll be up and around in another week. Just rest now."

Cameron heard footsteps leaving. The brightness still hammered at the far side of his eyelids. He turned his head sideways, the effort sending pain shooting up and down his spine. He opened his eyes. At first he saw only white; he peered into a pillow. Cameron turned his head back in the direction of the light. The actinic glare dazzled him but he saw the room beyond.

Robotic equipment filled the tiny compartment. He had been given over to machines. Cameron relaxed. He understood robots. He trusted them. They were his faithful servants. His. Only his.

He slipped into a quiet, restful sleep.

"Chairman Fremont sent me," the bulky, powerful man said without preamble. Cameron forced himself to turn to face Metchnikoff. The IM director had not learned to temper his harsh voice with honeyed words to soothe and

A PLAGUE IN PARADISE

lull before betrayal. This was his only failing, as far as Cameron knew.

"I can report to you without fear of breaching security?" Cameron asked, his voice soft and polite.

"Dammit, of course you can. Fremont is in poor health. He requested a full report of how badly you botched the distribution of the brain burners."

"I carried out my orders to the letter," snapped Cameron, tiring of Metchnikoff. "If you truly represented Fremont, you would know that." The sight of the powerful man's eyes narrowing told Cameron that Metchnikoff had not been sent; he was seeking information for his own use.

"He wanted Humbolt dead," Metchnikoff said, more to himself than to Cameron.

"I had hoped you would bring word of my election to the board of directors to replace the unfortunate and inept Mr. Humbolt," said Cameron. A buzzing in his ears and recurring dizziness prevented him from sitting up in the automated bed. Dozens of threadlike tubes fed him, removed bodily wastes, kept his immune system at a peak for the operation scheduled later this day.

Metchnikoff sneered. "You? On the board? Never!"

"It would be such a fine token of esteem from Chairman Fremont. Recognition of my services on Bizzie worlds." Cameron's eyes flickered slightly. A gnat-sized aerial robot that had been resting on the ceiling activated and became airborne. A second blink would send this minute assassin into Metchnikoff's ear. The robot had been ordered to use a tiny laser to drill through the eardrum and find its way into its victim's brain. There, it would do as much damage as possible until its power source failed.

Cameron estimated that it would need only microseconds to destroy Metchnikoff's brain. How dare he insult the man who had Fremont's complete trust!

Unless...

Cameron stirred and tried to sit up. Political changes occurred constantly on Gamma Tertius 4. Had Fremont's health failed to the point that the drugs that kept him alert and alive no longer worked? Fremont was a frail old man, but Cameron had not expected any major power shifts in the few weeks he had been stranded on the Bizzie planet.

"You're being operated on this afternoon?" asked Metchnikoff.

"There is still pressure on points in my brain. Internal bruises. Subdermal hemostasia."

"You will become brain damaged—dead—without the operation," Metchnikoff said, again as if thinking out loud.

"Why did you come to visit? Not to cheer me with your presence," snapped Cameron. He almost started his robotic killer toward Metchnikoff's ear. Metchnikoff threatened him; he could justify the director's death later.

"You assume too much, Cameron. You are not a director. IM needs your services, but in a lesser capacity."

"Fremont needed me."

"As a trained killer only. Jump through the hoop like a trained beast. Sit up, roll over, kill." Metchnikoff saw the sudden flash of hatred boil in Cameron's eyes. "Don't think to use your pitiful little robot on me."

Cameron blinked.

The gnat glinted in the actinic glare of the UV disinfectant light as it arrowed for Metchnikoff. It emitted a tiny *pop!* before it found its target. Metchnikoff had surrounded himself with a damping field that prevented the small robot from reaching him.

"Anything larger I can destroy in other ways," Metchnikoff said, sneering. "For instance, an emotionless robot like you. All I need to do is reach over and squeeze." Metchnikoff's heavy fingers closed on Cameron's windpipe. He struggled to pull the choking hands away but his strength fled quickly. From the corner of his eye Cameron saw red warning lights begin to flash. His vital signs faded.

The intense pressure on his throat eased but the hands remained. Through the thunder of blood pounding in his own ears, Cameron heard Metchnikoff say, "We can aid one another. There is no need for trust, just respect. You are good at what you do, but you can never assume a directorship. I'll see to that. But you can gain more than you have now, if we work together."

"Stop," moaned Cameron.

"Ah, he speaks. But does he listen? I think so. You, Cameron, are an expert killer. But you are mortal and can become the victim of your own clever mechanisms." The fingers tightened slightly, then relaxed. "You might die now and no one would question the cause of your death."

"What do you want, Metchnikoff?"

"Your cooperation. Fremont is ill much of the time. I need support to gain control of IM. I am going to be the next chairman of the company." Metchnikoff removed his strangling fingers and stepped back. "You can stand behind and help me, or stand in front of me and be crushed under my heel. Which is it to be?"

The room spun in ever-widening circles. Deep inside his brain Cameron felt horrible, numbing pressure mounting. His nose began to bleed and a black curtain pulled across Metchnikoff's leering face. Before he sank into unconsciousness, Cameron heard the emergency alarms ringing —his secretly installed emergency alarms.

Metchnikoff had disconnected the hospital's.

"You're looking better, Cameron," the tall, dark woman said. She peered down at him with cold, flinty eyes. Maria Villalobos perched on the edge of his bed, reminding Cameron of a vulture waiting for its dinner to die.

"The operation went well," he said.

"I spoke with the doctors. One was very annoyed that you insisted on having... protection during the operation."

"My robots didn't bother the surgeons. They insured my survival." Cameron smiled wickedly. If any of the doctors had attempted to let him die while on the operating table, his assassin robots would have ended the doctor's career quickly. He had not been hesitant about letting the men and women know that, either.

"I would not have let Metchnikoff murder you." Villalobos reached out and touched icy fingers to his cheek. "I still need you."

"Am I nothing more than a replaceable part in your machine?" he asked. Metchnikoff irritated him; Maria Villalobos fascinated him. Cameron had to admit to lust for the woman. What would she be like in bed? Could any man fire her passions or did Villalobos concentrate solely on rising in Interstellar Materials' power structure?

"You are more," she assured him, a touch of irony in her tone. "You performed admirably on ZOo. Humbolt never knew that Fremont ordered you to kill him."

"I could have done more about the brain burners if I'd been in charge. The arachnoid Bizzies will never allow IM on-planet again. We had a good chance to remove an entire planet of them and Humbolt allowed it to slip away."

"Humbolt was a fool."

"Why wasn't I elected to replace him on the board of directors?" Cameron swung his legs over the side of the bed. Most of the medical support tubes had been removed, and he felt more alive than he had since arriving home."

"Director Liu and I discussed the matter," Villalobos said, her cold, dark eyes unwavering. Cameron knew she could lie and never show even a small muscular twitch to betray herself, but he sensed that she spoke the truth this time. "We did not have the support to elect you."

"Am I obligated to Liu for this?"

"You never cared for Liu, I know," she said. Villalobos shook out her long, lustrous black hair and let it fall in a cascade of raven softness. She smiled. Cameron kept his breathing under control. The look in her eyes, the way her tongue delicately touched and wetted her lips, the set of her body, all promised more than an IM directorship.

Why? What did Maria Villalobos want from him? And would he give it?

Cameron walked around the small cubicle on weak legs. Strength returned slowly, but he hid his weakness from the woman. Like the others in the company, like all those who believed implicitly in the Stellar Death Plan, weakness was always rewarded with death.

He wanted more from her than a new way to die.

Some ingenious use of technology allowed the woman to open the tight collar of her severe suit without touching it. Cameron found it impossible not to watch the slow parting of the fabric as it revealed Villalobos' swanlike neck, the warm flesh of her chest, the valley between her breasts, the firm swells of her breasts.

"We needed to maintain a position of strength for a new project. I felt that any . . . extraneous matters might jeopardize efforts to further the Plan."

"A new assault on the Bizzies with the brain burners?"

"Something more," she said. Villalobos leaned back on the bed. The suit parted further, revealing more of a breast until a dark aureole showed. Cameron found it difficult to keep his mind on the woman's words rather than her body. How many others had she lured into such a trap? Many, he decided.

"You need me to assist in the field?"

"Something like that," she said. "This is a joint effort between several companies. You know how touchy such matters can become. Each has its own method for advancing the Stellar Death Plan. We have decided to abandon the Bizzie brain burners in favor of a different approach, a biological approach."

"One initiated by GPMT?" Cameron guessed.

"GPMT is involved slightly. Our direct contact is with Terra Recreations, however."

Cameron frowned. He did not understand how an entertainment conglomerate entered the grand scheme for the elimination of all aliens and their humiliating treatment of humans.

"Three companies makes it too involved."

Villalobos dismissed his objection with the wave of her hand. "You failed on ZOo. We have to find something other than the brain burners."

"*I* failed!" cried Cameron. "It was Humbolt. All Fremont asked of me was to remove Humbolt, and I did."

"Then there's the matter of Barton Kinsolving," she went on, as if she hadn't heard.

"He's dead. He could not have escaped my robot sentries."

"No body was found."

"I've seen the repots. The damned Bizarres prevented examination of the warehouse after they found Humbolt dead. IM personnel were barred from the entire planet."

"That's not important at the moment. I just wanted you to realize that there were reasons for the opposition to your election to the board." Villalobos swung her long, sleek legs up and rested fully on the bed. "Fremont would look upon your promotion favorably if we succeed in this new venture."

"What is it?" He found himself intrigued by the way her hem hiked up to mid thigh. It was almost as if neckline and hem were in a race to touch at her waist and leave her vulnerable and exposed.

If Maria Villalobos could ever be described as vulnerable.

"A virus that attacks only Bizzies. Our mines on Askerath produce the only mineral that the virus will incubate in. Once released, it destroys aliens but allows humans to mingle with the infected at no risk. When the last Bizzie is dead, the plague dies out."

"We can take over entire planets."

"IM will profit," she agreed. "And so can I. So can we. We're of a kind, Cameron, you and I."

He looked at her and the wanton lust in her eyes. The suit parted completely and left her seductively naked to the waist. The skirt began opening. For him.

"Fremont won't live forever. IM needs new strength," she said. "Strengths that we can give it."

Cameron sat on the bed, then allowed her to pull him down. Even though the operation had enervated him, Cameron discovered the strengths within himself that Villalobos spoke of.

She was everything he had imagined—and more.

CHAPTER THREE

"ISN'T IT SIMPLY PHOTONIC!" squealed Lark. She spun around, arms outstretched as she took in the immense Xanadu Suite. Kinsolving wondered what the Royal Suite looked like if this was a "lesser quality" room. "Watch me. You'll love this, Bart, darling."

Lark took a deep breath, composed herself, then ran and jumped onto the immense bed dominating the center of the room. She landed feetfirst on the bed and sprang into the air. Kinsolving took an involuntary step forward to catch her as she somersaulted through the air toward a bulkhead. He need not have bothered. Hidden lenses picked up her action and robotic controls whirred into quick motion to lower a soft pad on the wall.

Lark hit, squealed again with joy and bounced back. She landed on her feet and stumbled into Kinsolving's outstretched arms.

"We're watched constantly?" he asked. Kinsolving tried to find the vidcams and failed. They were expertly hidden.

"Anything you want, just ask. They listen and they'll deliver." To demonstrate, Lark said, "Food: something gooey and tasting good, like vanilla or *denba* spice, perhaps. And hot. I want it heat hot but not spice hot. No need to worry about protein and those dreary things. What else?" She looked at Kinsolving, who frowned. She kissed him and then ordered, "I want the food delivered. Now."

Kinsolving jerked about, Lark still hanging around his neck, to see a small door opening in the far bulkhead. A metal tray laden with steaming, aromatic food hovered on a magnetic field.

"See?" she said. "Anything you want. Anything."

Lark kissed him. He started to pull back, the thought of spying eyes making him uneasy. Lark prevented any such precipitous move. For several seconds, they kissed. She finally broke it off and looked up into his dark eyes, smiling broadly. "Let's eat!" Lithely, she spun from his arms and went to the food tray, took it and placed it on a more substantial table. Kinsolving joined her, his own enthusiasm for Almost Paradise not matching Lark's.

As he ate he carefully studied the sumptuous room. The decks were covered with soft, springy green fabric that, on first glance, looked like natural grass. No real growing plant, however, had ever been manicured into such perfection of texture and eye-soothing color. The oyster-white walls curved upward as if they sat within a real pleasure dome. Kinsolving almost expected Coleridge to enter and begin reciting his poem.

The furnishings were few but elegantly carved from natural woods. Some Kinsolving recognized. Others he guessed to be from alien worlds. Impossible to ignore was the circular bed with its twisted, white driftwood headboard and elaborately turned bedposts. Nowhere did he see a vidcamera or other electronics.

"I don't like the idea of someone spying on us all the time," he said.

"Oh, Bart, darling, you're such a black hole when it comes to these things. You can drain the good times away *so* fast. Why do you think anyone *cares* what we do or don't do? They are our servants, not our keepers."

Kinsolving did not dispute this, but other disquieting thoughts fleetingly crossed his mind. Had the work crews found Rani duLong's body in the vacuum coffin? The Lorr had proven more tenacious in their attempts to return him to the prison world than he'd have thought. He had injured their pride in being the only escapee. Should he expect them soon?

His mind took other turnings. Paradise catered to humans and aliens. If he grounded, he might be able to find an alien willing to argue his case with the Lorr. Cameron had killed the agent-captain. Kinsolving thought that he might have gained easy acquittal if he had realized the gravity of his position—and that Interstellar Materials plotted against him because they needed a scapegoat.

Damn the Stellar Death Plan and all those working for its brutal ends!

"Are we allowed to talk to the other guests?"

"Here in Almost Paradise?" asked Lark around a mouthful of food.

He nodded. "Or down on-planet."

"Anything that spins your rotor. Paradise is a *pleasure* planet. They cater to your every whim."

He smiled at her. How lovely she looked. The faint pinkish glow in her cheeks might come from the cosmetic dyes injected beneath her skin or from true excitement. He didn't care. Lark Versalles was exotic and innocent, sophisticated—a gorgeous package of contradictions.

"You're all the whim I need," he said.

"Why, thank you, Barton. No man has ever said anything quite that nice to me before." She smiled wickedly. "But then, you haven't been to Paradise yet. You might find amusements that make me pale in comparison."

"I doubt it."

"Wait," she said. "I never tire of the world. Anything you want, really want deep down inside, is yours. They always seem to know and give it to you."

Again Kinsolving twitched at the idea of being under constant surveillance. "Let's explore," he said, pushing away from the meal. Kinsolving had eaten little of the tasty food, yet found himself completely sated. Such a miracle product would have brought billions on the commercial market. Starships had little room for storage, yet often required vast quantities of food and water for the crews and passengers. Reducing the bulk of edibles might allow larger engines and faster travel times.

Kinsolving shook his head sadly. Even increasing the speed of a human starship by fifty percent would still make them seem like snails against the alien stargoing vessels. The aliens used a different drive mechanism, a different mathematics to thwart the speed limit of light—and they refused to share the secret with any human.

Sometimes, in the dim, distant recesses of his mind, Kinsolving wondered why he opposed IM and Chairman Fremont and the others. The aliens *did* treat Earth as a second-rate world. They *did* sneer at humans as being less than civilized.

But Kinsolving had seen the nobility among them. They did not deserve to be eradicated totally. No man, no company, no species should be allowed to obliterate entire worlds. The Stellar Death Plan evoked genocide, not cooperation. Those twisted minds conceiving of the Plan had refused to see that humanity was a recent addition to starfaring races. Hard work, winning confidence, improvement in all areas, those were the entry codes to the aliens' universe, not death and mass destruction. The one professor that had influenced him the most in college, Dr. Delgado, had been positive that mankind would one day be accepted as an equal.

Kinsolving believed that.

"You look distant, Bart. Are you feeling ill? Sometimes the air in Almost Paradise is changed to accommodate other races. Why, I can't say, but it is."

"I'm fine," he assured her. "Let's explore."

Lark grabbed his hand and pulled him behind her like a small child trailing his mother. "You'll *love* it. But don't get too attached. There's so much more to do on-planet. This is just the appetizer before the main course."

Kinsolving blinked as Lark led him along the curving corridors of the space station. He might have walked into a museum. Masterpieces from a score of worlds decorated the bulkheads. He could barely get Lark to pause and look at some. The old Earth polages done by an artist named Austine particularly impressed him.

"These are fabulous," he said. "I've seen similar work on Earth, but nothing this fine."

"Oh, Bart, darling, this is *nothing*. Come on!"

She tugged and he followed, his eyes lingering on the flowing, changing images and colors of the polarized montages. When they emerged into a large common room, he caught his breath and held it. Never had Kinsolving seen such grandeur. The ceiling had been removed—or so it seemed. The vast star-dotted Milky Way arced across the room, undimmed by atmosphere or light pollution. Just staring at the stars would have satisfied him, but the room held so much more.

"Anything you want, Barton, anything," Lark whispered. He shared her reverential attitude. It seemed a blasphemy to speak in normal tones in this room. The artwork dotting the room had come from myriad worlds. Even in the largest of Earth's museums he had never seen such artistry and genius.

"The finest creators in the galaxy have contributed to this display," came a soft voice at his elbow. Kinsolving jumped, startled from his rapt appreciation. The woman behind him took away speech. Lark Versalles was gorgeous. This woman was . . . more.

It took him several seconds to understand why. He turned wary when he decided where he had seen her before. She looked a great deal like Ala Markken, his lover, his betrayer. Ala had allowed Cameron to implicate him in the murder on Deepdig. Ala had tried to kill him in the mines. Ala had become a conspirator in the Stellar Death Plan.

Barton Kinsolving still loved her. And before him was a woman who touched him with the subtle but powerful similarity in their appearances.

Lark tugged at his arm and whispered, "Who is she supposed to be?"

"What?" he said, startled at the question.

"They've run a memory scan on you. She must mean something to you or they wouldn't have taken the trouble to—"

"She's been made up to look like Ala!" he exclaimed. "They made her up?"

"Ala," said Lark, as if the name burned her tongue. "Very common name." Lark turned and wandered off before Kinsolving could stop her.

"Who are you?" he demanded of the woman who looked subtly like Ala Markken.

"Whoever you want me to be. Call me Sheeda."

"Is that your name? Or did you adopt it like you did that face?" He spoke sharply and immediately regretted it.

"Don't be cruel to me," Sheeda said, tears forming at the corners of her soft brown eyes. "I meant no harm. They told me you would be pleased."

"They don't know me well enough." Kinsolving touched his forehead as if he expected to find electrodes attached.

"Almost Paradise tries to give the guest whatever he wants most. I've failed. They . . . they won't be pleased with me."

"Wait," Kinsolving said, stopping the woman as she turned to leave. "What will they do to you?"

"Nothing."

"You're lying." He lifted her firm chin and stared into the oddly tinted eyes. Something about them struck him as wild—and not quite human. For all the facial similarities to Ala, the differences overwhelmed them now that he looked closely. Soft waves of brunette hair fell away from Sheeda's face in the same style that Ala wore, but the texture lacked luster.

The human luster.

"No," Sheeda said softly. "I am not human."

"What!" Kinsolving started. He bit back the demeaning question and started over. "Which planet do you call home?"

"We're not supposed to speak of such matters. I am hired to be for you and nothing more. Many humans do not like the idea of . . ." Sheeda's voice trailed off.

"Of a chameleon alien assuming the shape of a loved one?" Kinsolving shared that distaste, but he could not fault Sheeda for what the owners of Paradise considered normal treatment of guests. She was as much a victim as he was of the cruel masquerade.

"I am from the world we call Onar."

"Never heard of it."

"Most humans haven't," Sheeda said. A sibilance in her words again shook Kinsolving. Ala never spoke this way. But Sheeda from Onar did.

"Are you a chameleon or did they perform surgery to . . . to achieve this face?"

"I have limited muscular control over my features. All Onarians do. It makes life interesting being with us. We can do things no other race can." Sheeda pressed close. He caught the faint, sweet, exciting scent she wore. Kinsolving took a half step back; he recognized the aphrodisiac and was unprepared to deal with the consequences.

"Are you sending me back?"

"You said they'd punish you."

"Demote me. Terra Recreations is not a cruel employer. I have worked hard to achieve the status of entertainer. I began work on Almost Paradise as a shipboard helper."

Kinsolving looked around the room, pulling his attention away from the starry rainbow above him and the eerie feeling that he stood exposed to the harsh infinity of space.

He caught sight of Lark with a pair of men across the room. She laughed and clung to one man, her cosmetic dyes flowing in patterns Kinsolving made out even at this distance. He had seen such complexity in her before. Lark Versalles had again found her element and enjoyed herself immensely.

"Do you know other aliens?" he asked. "Captain Luxor said that a conference was in progress on-planet."

"Do you . . . prefer aliens to those of your kind? You are not the first," Sheeda said, "but it is the first time I have ever heard a human so openly state this preference."

"Not sexually," Kinsolving said quickly. "I want to talk to them. I need to explain certain things to someone with influence."

"There are several ambassadors meeting."

"The Trekan ambassador is in the Royal Suite," Kinsolving said. "Tell me about him."

Sheeda shrugged. "I know little of Treka. My specialty is Earth. Few of your kind detect the differences so quickly. Few want to. It is better to relax and indulge your fantasies. I am expert at that." She drew long fingers along Kinsolving's cheek. Again he caught the aphrodisiac scent of her perfume. That chemical stimulus with the closeness to Ala's appearance should have been enough. Kinsolving thought for most men coming to Paradise that it would be.

Under other circumstances, it would have been true paradise for him, too. But not now. Time worked against him. He needed to warn others of the Stellar Death Plan. Only when the aliens truly believed that IM controlled resources capable of clandestinely destroying entire worlds would he be free of his burden.

Such an alliance might even be adequate to clear him of the Lorr murder conviction.

"How do I meet the Trekan ambassador?" he asked.

"He is undergoing acclimation therapy to prepare him for on-planet meetings," Sheeda said. "It might be an intrusion into his fantasy to introduce a human."

"But you'll do it?" He saw the flow of emotion across Sheeda's face as she wrestled with the moral dilemma.

"I am entrusted with pleasing you, but I cannot displease another in doing so."

"Show me to the Royal Suite. Nothing more. Let me

assume all responsibility." Kinsolving glanced back at Lark, who had forgotten him. She and the two men had sunk down to a soft couch. Kinsolving couldn't tell what they were doing, but a long, naked leg kicked lightly in the air—Lark's.

"If that is your wish, I will do it."

They walked along the art-strewn corridors until Kinsolving got lost in the complex maze. It seemed that every few meters a connecting shaft joined the main hall at a strange angle. The station's curvature also added a dimension to his confusion until he relied solely on Sheeda's homing instincts.

She stopped suddenly. A brief frown crossed her face. "There," she said. "The door with the engraved platinum studs. The Trekan ambassador is within."

"Thank you. There's no need to wait," he said, "unless you want to." Kinsolving was not sure if he wanted Sheeda waiting for him or not. A part of him begged for her to agree, to give even tacit support. Another part told him that she might find herself in deep trouble if his unannounced meeting did not fare well.

"I'd best leave," she said. In that moment she both looked and sounded exactly like Ala Markken. A lump formed in Kinsolving's throat. He nodded briskly, then left her in the center of the corridor.

He stood before the platinum-studded door, his hand almost touching the annunciator. Every second would count if the Trekan allowed him an interview. He had no idea how the alien would respond to his story—or if the ambassador would even listen. Kinsolving swallowed hard. He knew little about Treka and relied only on the being's position. Anyone sent as an ambassador had to have some standing in the alien community.

Kinsolving faced the prospect of the alien immediately summoning the Lorr to return him to the prison world.

He knew the risk and had to take it. Alerting the aliens to the potential evil of the Plan outweighed all personal considerations. He could not allow billions of intelligent beings to perish because of bigotry.

He touched the annunciator and heard a faint chiming deep within the suite. At the same instant he caught a reflection off the polished surface of a door stud.

Kinsolving spun and ducked—too late. A heavy blow struck him on the side of the head. He sank to his knees, turning enough to avoid a second blow. He lifted arms that had turned to lead. A kick landed squarely in his belly. As he doubled over a third blow crunched into the base of his skull. The universe again became populated with blazing stars.

Then all slipped into velvet blackness.

CHAPTER FOUR

BARTON KINSOLVING moaned and tried to roll onto his back to ease the pressure on his neck. He moved but the pain increased. He lifted his hand and banged it against a hard surface. Slowly forcing away the pain and trying not to panic, he opened his eyes. Dim light filtered through a vent set high on the bulkhead providing barely enough illumination to see. He reached out and ran his hands along the walls.

He found no opening. Stifling the waves of red pain washing through his head and body, he turned and sat with his back against one cool wall. He could not stretch out his legs in the cramped compartment. Forcing his feet out, he squirted himself up to a standing position. The chamber proved hardly wider than his shoulders but much higher than he could reach.

Kinsolving jumped, trying to grab the vent and pull himself up to peer out. He missed by centimeters. A second jump failed by even more. His strength faded fast. Panting, he bent forward, hands on knees. His head rested against the cool bulkhead.

"What is this place?" he wondered aloud. After he recovered, he tried once more. This time his stubby fingers found a grip on the vent grill. Kinsolving kicked and struggled and pulled himself up. He looked out into a larger compartment filled with heavy machinery. It took him several seconds to identify the waste disposal equipment.

His fingers began to throb with the pain of supporting his entire weight. Kinsolving gritted his teeth and shook the vent as hard as he could, trying to dislodge it. All he accomplished was losing his grip and tumbling back into the small chamber.

Kinsolving had been a mining engineer most of his adult life. The equipment outside he recognized as providing the gaseous and solid waste disposal for Almost Paradise. The function of the compartment he found himself trapped in proved too esoteric. He had no clue to its purpose, even after examining it carefully.

His fingers found a small elastomer air seal at the bottom of the chamber, and he thought he saw a similar seal around the ceiling but it was too high for him to be certain.

"Someone put me in here. No doors or other apparent openings except for the vent. That's got to be the way out." Kinsolving decided to worry about who had attacked him later. If he failed to escape, this tiny compartment might become his coffin. He had no food or water and, although the air coming through the vent seemed adequate, the seal at the bottom of the chamber worried him. Engineers never put in seals unless they were needed.

Jumping again gained him a view out into the equipment room. He shouted to attract attention. His cries were drowned by the bull-throated rumbles of the equipment as it worked. His fingers began to slip and cramp again. Kinsolving worked them deeper into the vent's mesh grill. He didn't want to injure those fingers; bloodied, they would turn slippery and prevent him from hanging on for more than a few seconds.

He pressed his face against the grill and tried to study the machinery closer to the bulkhead. He blanched when he saw the multiloader next to the vent. Kinsolving dropped back to the floor of his small chamber.

The loader filled his tiny prison with one of three kinds of waste: solid, liquid or gaseous. After spewing forth the waste, a special door sealed the loading vent—his only view to the exterior—and then? Almost Paradise evacuated its debris into space, probably toward the planet's atmosphere.

After the garbage jetted out it would enter the upper atmosphere and burn. Kinsolving had nothing to worry about on that score. He would die from lack of oxygen and the effects of hard vacuum before he incinerated.

He jumped up and began shouting again. "Let me out. Somebody, let me out!"

The hum of robot-controlled machinery rose until it became a scream over which he could never shout. To his horror he saw the protective grate pulling back. He leaped and caught the edge of the now-open vent—and got a smelly stream of semiliquid waste in the face for his effort.

Kinsolving grimly clung to the edge of the vent. He tried to pull himself up and force his body through the opening against the stream. He quickly found that the hose mechanism on the loader prevented this. His shoulders were too large to cram into the loader.

His fingers slipped and he dropped back into the tiny waste disposal chamber. But this time he did not reach the floor. Buoyed by the sewage, he floated a meter under the vent opening. Floundering about, he caught the edge of the opening again in time to see the grill descending. He kicked hard and screamed to give himself the extra strength.

His shoulders and upper body passed through the opening as the grill lowered. Kinsolving screamed in pain. The closing mechanism had not been set to react to blockage; it would mindlessly try to shut the grill no matter what it encountered.

His head had rammed deep into the noisome loader. He could go no further.

And in this Kinsolving found salvation. Small sensors ringed the loader hose to measure back pressure. He shoved his hand against a piezoelectric sensing crystal as hard as he could. Nothing. Kinsolving dragged his fingernail over the surface.

As he felt his grip slipping, his body sliding back into the sewage in the chamber, he heard a distant alarm ringing. It might bring a human to investigate. More likely, a repair robot would be dispatched to clear what it sensed as blockage.

Grimly, Kinsolving hung on. When the loader hose pulled back, he gasped. The edge of the vent caught him just under his arms and placed most of his weight on a sharp edge. He grabbed the loader hose and, as it retreated, let it pull him up and out of the disposal chamber.

He fell heavily to the floor. Kinsolving lay there gasping for breath and choking on the sewage. Alarms stopped ringing. The grill clanged shut. A pressure seal swung down and closed over it with a lewd sucking sound. He heard pumps start as the disposal chamber was highly pressurized. Getting up on shaky legs, he found that the floor was much higher on this side and that the grill was at eye level. Kinsolving pressed his face against the transparent pressure seal and watched.

He jumped away, startled, when the bottom of the chamber opened. Like a gas-powered rocket, the sewage shot from the chamber. The liquid boiled away almost instantly, freezing the sewage into a compact missile shape. Kinsolving saw the bottom of the chamber return and he lost sight of the sewage, now on its way to a fiery destruction in Paradise's atmosphere.

Turning, he slipped down the opposite side of the bulkhead from where he had been trapped and simply sat, numb and unable to think.

Death had been very close. But why? Who wanted to kill him like this? He saw how efficient the disposal of his corpse would have been. No trace would have remained.

"What the hell kind of pervo are you?" demanded a burly man in coveralls. He had come to check the waste loader. "I seen all kinds on this floating whorehouse but you're at the outer boundary. Wallowing in shit. Damnation!"

Kinsolving forced himself to stand. He shrugged his shoulders, winced at the pain, and said, "Don't complain until you try it."

"Damned Bizzies are easier to tolerate than the likes of you," the man said, eyes cold and face set in an unpleasant expression. "You damage my equipment?"

"Who else has access to this room?"

"Get the hell out of my sight!" the man roared. "I don't want you bringing pervo friends in here. Out!"

Kinsolving followed the direction the man pointed. Dripping sewage, he found a door leading to a gray-painted service corridor. He stopped to wipe off the worst of the sewage, but he knew he did a poor job. Walking through the elegant Almost Paradise would draw unwanted attention.

A small box mounted on the wall drew his attention. He opened it and heaved a sigh of relief. A com unit. Kinsolving pushed his thumb into the button and waited.

"How may we be of service, sir?" came a soft, sultry voice.

"Lark Versalles. I want to talk with her right away."

"I am sorry, sir, but Lark left orders that no one is to disturb her."

"I'm Barton—"

"Barton Kinsolving," the voice interrupted. "Yes, sir, we know." Kinsolving cursed under his breath. Of course they knew. Their damned vidcams were everywhere—except in the waste disposal compartment.

Or were they even there? Had he been watched? Thoughts of insane bets among the guests on Almost Paradise ran through his mind. Bets on whether he survived, whether he escaped within an allotted time, bets on how soon he turned to ash in the atmosphere after being ejected into space.

"Sheeda. Send Sheeda to me."

"Of course, sir."

Kinsolving lifted his thumb from the bottom and sagged against the wall. Anger burned bright at the center of his being and kept him from succumbing to the darkness trying to seize his mind.

"Barton?" came Sheeda's hesitant question. "Are you all right? What have you been doing?"

He looked around. The alien woman stared at him as if he had fallen into a barrel of shit. And he had.

"Get me back to my room without anyone else seeing me."

"Another guest?"

"Of course," he snapped. "Do you think I want to be seen like this?"

"There are many strange customs, even stranger pleasures. I have read about—"

"Sheeda," he interrupted, "my room. Now."

The alien woman motioned for him to follow. He saw her pert nose wrinkle at the odor and she danced away lightly as he reached to touch her arm.

In silence they went along sharply curving corridors. Kinsolving tried to imagine their route. His only guess was that they followed the outermost passages and avoided the central areas where the guests congregated. His relief was infinite when they came to the door of the Xanadu Suite.

"Do you want me to join you?" Sheeda asked, obviously hoping for a negative reply.

"I have some questions. Nothing more." Kinsolving

pushed into the room, stripping off his clothing as he went. Sheeda closed the door behind them and motioned. Obedient, silent ankle-high robots slipped from their stations along the walls and retrieved his clothing. Kinsolving didn't care where they took it. Let it be exhausted into space for all it mattered.

"Bath, on, maximum pleasure," Sheeda said. "For one."

Kinsolving stepped into the filling bath and discarded the last of his soiled clothes. Slipping down into the scented cleaning fluid gave a surge of pleasure that was almost sexual. He moved his hand over a nearby control. Tiny scrubbers began working on his body as the warm pink fluid continuously circulated.

"Sheeda, what happened when you left me at the door to the ambassador's suite?"

"I watched for a second, then went to report in person to my supervisor. I had displeased you in some way and needed further instructions."

"You didn't displease me," Kinsolving said. The soft scrubbing had stopped. New sensations replaced it. Tingling electric current flowed to relax his tensed muscles. Fresh fluids gushed into the tub. This time his scrapes and abrasions were treated by astringents. He relaxed even more, almost drifting off to sleep.

But he dared not relax too much. Not until he figured out what had happened when he had approached the Trekan ambassador.

"I'm glad," Sheeda said, sitting on the edge of the tub. Her fingers stroked his face.

"You didn't see who hit me?"

"What?" She jerked back, as if he had struck her. "No, I didn't know. Is *that* what happened to you?"

"Someone knocked me unconscious, then put me in a waste disposer."

"That's not possible."

"Every guest is watched closely. That means someone in your central control knows exactly what happened." Even as he spoke, he wondered if the person responsible for trying to kill him was listening... and plotting.

"That's not exactly true," Sheeda said. "Guests are not constantly monitored. If you speak certain words a computer interprets it as a request and takes appropriate action. There is no need to watch everyone. The robots and computers do much of the work. Mechanisms are not as likely as humans to be inattentive."

"Then it's possible that no one saw my attacker."

"You are so suspicious, Barton. We on Almost Paradise do not spy, we assist. Very seldom is there any violence. Why bother, when anything you want is given freely?"

Kinsolving said nothing. He had known men and women who thrived on violence. The act of hurting excited them. As complete as Terra Recreations seemed, he did not doubt that Paradise contained a special section for sadists.

His attacker, though, did not seem to be in that category of guest. He had tried to remove all trace of Kinsolving's body. Knowledge of the station's workings were needed. Kinsolving could have hunted for a month without finding the disposal equipment.

"Someone on the staff did it," he said, "not a guest."

"But why?"

Kinsolving did not answer the Onarian's simple question directly. He had not decided if he trusted her. Complicating his decision was her uncanny resemblance to Ala Markken. He had trusted Ala. Trusting another who looked so much like her might have been logical but emotionally presented huge barriers for him.

"None of the guests knew I was aboard the station. Only the staff could have seen me."

"That doesn't answer the question of motive," she said. "Did you book passage to Paradise so long ago that such a plot could be woven against you?"

"No," he said slowly. His mind raced ahead, checking possibilities and not liking them. "Someone acted on impulse. That means they recognized me."

"Are you such a desperate creature that our staff attacks on sight?" The idea amused Sheeda. The corners of her mouth turned up in a crinkly smile the same as Ala's.

He considered the elements of the attack. Someone might have wanted to keep him from the Trekan ambassador. A guard? A more straightforward warning would have sufficed. A Lorr police officer had no reason to stuff him in the sewage. A prison world waited for him if the aliens caught him. Had a repair crewman found Rani duLong's body, recognized her—a former lover?—and vowed vengeance? That seemed too nebulous a reason.

Not many capable of such an attack remained except those involved with the Stellar Death Plan.

Not Cameron, he decided. The robot master had died or been so severely injured that he would never recover—Kinsolving hoped. If only he could have made sure of Cameron's condition!

Another in Interstellar Materials might have stumbled onto him. Director Liu had ample reason to attack him. Others working for IM and the Plan might also kill on sight—would kill, he amended. The method of attack, though, did not seem efficient enough.

"What about Lark?" he asked. "Where is she?"

"Enjoying herself. As you should do. This is Almost Paradise." Sheeda stroked his cheek, then pulled back damp fingers to begin unfastening her blouse.

"I want to go to Paradise," he said.

"Let me begin giving it to you here," Sheeda said, smiling broadly. She shucked off her blouse and began working on her slacks. As she stepped out of them, Kinsolving went pale.

"You," he sputtered. "You're—"

"I am Onarian," Sheeda said. "Does my sexual equipment not please you?"

"You're not a woman!"

"But I am," Sheeda said, chuckling at his confusion. "I am also a man. I am both. I can fulfill any need."

Kinsolving jerked away and grabbed a robe brought by a convenience robot. He stared at Sheeda. She is not human, he repeated over and over to himself. It did not help. Sheeda had both male and female genitalia. In a detached fashion, he saw how this made her a valuable asset to TR and the guests on Almost Paradise.

That did nothing to ease the discomfort he felt at being in her/his presence.

"I want to go to Paradise. When will I be able to leave?"

"Soon," Sheeda said. The Onarian quickly dressed and hurried to the door. Kinsolving saw the bright beads of tears in Sheeda's eyes caused by his rejection. "I will expedite your departure since there is nothing on Almost Paradise that pleases you."

Sheeda rushed from the room before he could explain. Kinsolving dropped to the bed and lay back, trying to pull all the jagged pieces of his life together. He finally gave up, realizing that he couldn't explain his reaction to Sheeda. He might not possess the xenophobia of those adhering to the Stellar Death Plan, but he was not a sophisticated traveller, either.

He was only a bumpkin from a backward Earth. Kinsolving vowed to apologize to Sheeda for his behavior, but he didn't have the slightest idea how he would do it.

CHAPTER FIVE

CAMERON SHIFTED his weight slowly. A small buzzing in his ears told him that he had not yet adjusted the automedic properly. His injuries were healed satisfactorily, but he took no chances with his health. The robotic guardian rested in the hollow under his left ear and monitored his brainwave patterns. Should any discrepancy between norm and observed frequency occur, it would alert him.

The human doctors on Gamma Tertius 4 had scoffed at him and his precautions. Although they had repaired him, he did not trust them. A part of him said that the doctors might have made major mistakes if he had not posted his robot killers in the operating room to oversee the delicate procedure. The doctors had taken over four hours to drill through his skull with a laser, find the clots threatening his life and remove them from his brain. At every stage his robot observers compared the results with optimum. Cameron had gone over their detailed reports; twice the doctors had deviated from the best possible course, only to be warned by the observant robots.

Cameron touched the automedic and worked at its minute controls until the buzzing vanished. He had worried needlessly about the device during the shift to Paradise. It had performed perfectly in hyperspace. Not even the increased atmospheric pressure and higher humidity aboard ship had affected the sensitive warning device.

"Mr. Cameron, a pleasure," greeted a Terra Recreations representative. The man had the look of a petty bureaucrat about him that immediately caused Cameron to dislike him. Maria Villalobos had sent him to this resort planet for a purpose. Filling out endless reports to be hidden away in obscure computer banks was not part of his mission.

"I'm to see Morgan Suarez," he said without responding to the man's outstretched hand.

"Dr. Suarez is, uh, in his lab." The man looked around, as if saying even this much in public might be a mistake.

"Then there is nothing for me to do but wait for him." Cameron smiled, his gray eyes as cold as polar ice. "I do not like to wait. I get nervous. When I get nervous, I kill things."

The TR agent had no doubt about what—whom—Cameron meant when he said "things."

"Dr. Suarez will be available in a few hours. Why, uh, don't you amuse yourself? Paradise is famous for its many diversions." The sweat beading on the man's forehead betrayed his discomfort at having to deal with Cameron. In a way, this pleased Cameron.

"At least you didn't force me to wait on the space station." He glanced up and saw a silvery dot in the azure sky. Cameron had been granted direct landing clearance, spending less than fifteen minutes aboard Almost Paradise before shuttling down. He wondered who among those on Paradise were adherents to the Stellar Death Plan. Most employees of Terra Recreations knew nothing, just as most of those working for Interstellar Materials had never even heard of the Plan. Companies had to make money to justify their existence. The Plan provided an added bonus for company and employee worthy of the knowledge.

Cameron could not hold back the involuntary shudder that shook him when he thought of the Bizarres and how they crushed mankind under their alien heel. He lacked altruistic purpose, but the end benefited humanity. Cameron could not bear the thought of being second-rate. Having Bizzies constantly tell him by word and deed of his human frailty and inferior intellect produced nothing but gut-churning need to excel.

"Are you all right, Mr. Cameron?"

"Not used to the planet yet," he lied. "I've been in space for some time."

"You were in TR's flagship," the man said, perplexed. "There's nothing faster out there, except for alien vessels, of course."

"Of course," Cameron said sarcastically. The TR ship had cut over a month of travel time off the GT4–Paradise route. A Bizzie ship—any Bizzie ship—shifted the same distance in one percent of the time. What humans measured in weeks and months, the damned Bizzies measured in minutes and hours.

"May I show you to your quarters?" the man asked. "We've followed your request and given you something out of the way, a small bungalow that isn't likely to be noticed."

"And the equipment?"

"It's already inside," the man said, motioning for Cameron to precede him along a small, winding, dirt path. Cameron strode off, confident that the man would not attempt to kill him. A dozen gnat-sized robots patrolled the path, each capable of stopping an assassin silently and quickly. All had been redesigned after his encounter with Metchnikoff to penetrate personal defensive screens, but to make certain of his own invincibility, Cameron carried four different devices, all programmed for self-defense and given autonomy to prevent any attack. The AI circuits had performed even better than Cameron had expected when he had tested them on GT4. Anything the robots could not kill outright they could outsmart.

"No insects," he observed. "Yet there are colored flowers. How do the plants reproduce?"

"All artificial, sir," the man said. "We've found that the buzzing of insects distracts many guests. Others fear insect bites."

"Fear? Isn't that a strong word to use for a minor annoyance?"

"No, sir," the guide said, warming to a safe topic. "Some arrive with immune system responses not geared to the native insects. Anaphylactic shock is certainly something to fear for many. On Paradise, our guests are shielded, and so there is nothing to fear. That makes it perfect for both human and nonhuman vacationers."

"Nonhuman," mused Cameron. "Are these Bizzies on Paradise now?"

"Usually, as much as fifteen percent of the total clientele is alien," the man said, obviously distressed at the pejorative term Cameron used.

"All planets? Lorr? Zeta Orgo 4?"

"We've never had any arachnoids. They stay close to Web. The Lorr are infrequent visitors. Currently, we have a large contingent of Trekans and six other species comprising the Lemma Cluster Confederation."

"A large Bizzie trade group," Cameron said, more to himself than to the guide.

"Yes, sir, one of the largest in all space. Here is your bungalow. If you should require anything larger, we can accommodate you." The man bustled about, pointing out the automated features. To Cameron they were almost laughably primitive. The simplest of his robots performed more tasks—and better. Quick hand gestures dispatched six of his aerial guardians to perform a complete scan of the small house. Before the TR guide had finished his sales talk, Cameron saw the flicker of a green light from the coordinator robot.

No hidden traps.

"You requested isolation mode," the man droned on. "If you require anything, you must toggle the com unit. Minimum response on Paradise is full verbal. We could then cater to your needs whenever you—"

"I need privacy, not instant service," Cameron said. He turned and moved the man toward the door. "Thank you for your time. Send a message when Suarez is available."

"Yes, sir. Would you prefer to see the resort director? Dr. Suarez might be some time. Supervisor Azmotega would be thrilled to meet someone of your obvious distinction."

"I have no need to see the director." Cameron shut the door and prevented any further blithering. He had arrived without notifying any but a handful of TR personnel. Although the arrival of TR's flagship would cause gossip, his quick transfer to the planet kept such talk to a minimum. Cameron wondered at TR's efficiency. His officious guide obviously knew certain elements of the Plan and Suarez's part in it, yet Cameron had been told that Supervisor Azmotega knew nothing—of the Plan, of Suarez's mission, of his own arrival.

He glanced around. The protective robots had positioned themselves in each of the room's four upper corners. Two others patrolled constantly. He went into the bedroom and found his requested equipment neatly packed in shipping crates. Cameron began unfastening the lids.

"This is more like it." The equipment set his heart

pounding a little faster. The automedic beeped a single warning, then realized that its human ward experienced only excitement, not distress. Cameron had been cooped up in the hospital for almost a week after the operation. The time spent in transit had worn on him, too, but he had not felt secure enough aboard the TR ship to work.

With tools such as the ones contained in the crates, he could again work robotic miracles of miniaturization. Cameron wasted no time setting up a worktable, the automated equipment carefully positioned around him. Within an hour he had fashioned a new and even more deadly aerial robot.

Back hurting, he leaned against the pneumatic chair support. Cameron stretched. Warm, syrupy gold sunlight slanted through the bedroom window. Cameron shook his head. He had been so intent on his work that he had forgotten to polarize the window to prevent unwanted spying.

"Getting careless," he said. He checked his patrolling sentries. They had not detected any spying activities, but optical observation from a distance was beyond their programming to notice. "Damned planet is too quiet. Lulls me."

Cameron did not want to admit that his head injuries might have affected him adversely. Better to claim a moment's inattention than to believe in a more permanent condition of sloppiness.

He carefully repacked the micromanipulators and made certain that anyone looking at the electronic remains on the worktable would be unable to determine the purpose of his project. Cameron held out his hand. Obediently, the aerial robot he had constructed whipped up and off the table and gently settled in his palm. He dropped a pair of magnifiers down over his eyes and examined the new creation critically.

Only when he was sure that it would do its task well did he remove the magnifiers. A slow smile crossed his lips. It had been some time since he had felt this good. Paradise was already working its subtle charm on him.

Cameron rose, checked his robotic sentries, then left the small house and walked briskly along the tiny dirt path. When he had gone fifty meters, he cut off the trail and plunged into the thicket. Cameron ignored the small cuts and scrapes he got from the tough vegetation. His course began to curve slightly. From a map he had seen and memorized he headed directly for an alien compound.

A sharp crack alerted him. A robot guard that patrolled ahead had found sensors. Approaching more deliberately, Cameron found what his robot had already discovered. He dropped to his knees and examined the sensor head carefully. It had IR and vid pickups, both temporarily scrambled by his robot's defensive EM field. Cameron might have sent his messenger of death on ahead and returned to his bungalow without dealing with the warning device himself.

He wanted to witness personally the death delivered by his new robot.

Agile fingers worked on the leads. In less than a minute Cameron had circumvented a sophisticated warning device. He connected a small box to the output wire. A few seconds later, the repeater had photographed the harmless vegetation and transmitted this false picture endlessly to anyone monitoring the sensor.

Confident, Cameron strode forward. From inside the Bizzie compound he heard snuffling and grunting.

"The Bizzies are feeding," he said softly to the small robot in his hand. "Help them diet—permanently."

Cameron put on a set of vid goggles. Through the clear part of the lenses he saw the alien compound. By slightly unfocusing his eyes, he got a view of the aerial robot's journey inward. It flew slowly, barely fast enough for its tiny ramjet to keep it aloft. Cameron began retreating. The robot worked well so far in eluding the various detectors the Bizzies had placed for their safety.

Safety! With his skill, no Bizzie could ever be safe! Let them run, let them hide. He would ferret them out and destroy every last one of their kind!

Cameron watched his robot slide past the electrostatic shield intended to keep annoying insects away. As his robot encountered this electronic barrier, he frowned.

A blinding light blossomed in the vid goggles. It took Cameron several seconds to realize that the dazzling brilliance came from the robot's camera and not from a physical presence. He hastened back to the path and strolled along it until his vision cleared.

He almost laughed out loud when he figured out what had happened. The tiny dot of artificial intelligence he had given the robot had saved it. It now hunted the alien occupant.

Cameron walked faster. It would not do if he were seen near the scene of an alien death. Terra Recreations would shield him to a point. Cameron had yet to learn who among the officials on Paradise knew of the Plan and would aid him. The planetary supervisor knew nothing but Morgan Suarez definitely did, if the man would ever deign to grant an audience. Cameron smiled crookedly. Let Suarez fiddle in his bio lab with weapons of subtle—and mass—destruction. Cameron fantasized billions of his little robots being loosed on a Bizzie world. No alien would survive. If the robots maintained a modicum of intelligence, they could outsmart any alien. He proved that.

His eyes had cleared completely and the robot sent him a picture that caused his heart to race. A loud buzz sounded in his ear. The automedic warned him of undue excitement. Cameron ignored it. This was the moment he sought so avidly.

Robot life against inhuman life.

Cameron could not keep the smile from spreading when he watched his minuscule machine center its sights on the alien. The Bizarre crouched, six-fingered hands outstretched, as if this would save it. The sudden change in perspective caused Cameron to wobble slightly and grab a tree trunk for support. The robot had lined up its target. Program conditions met, it expended all its propellant in a single strike. It arrowed directly into the Bizzie's chest.

Cameron knew the alien hardly felt the impact of the tiny laser drilling through arteries and organs once it penetrated the body cavity. All transmission from the robot ceased. Cameron took off the vid goggles and put them in his pocket. He knew that by now the robot had probably found the gut and raced along it, seeking out vital organs and burning through them with the minute laser. The power supply could last only a few seconds at this level of energy expenditure.

Losing the robot did not sadden Cameron. He rejoiced at the death of another hated alien.

"Mr. Cameron?" came a gravelly voice.

Cameron's fingers moved in an almost imperceptible pattern. A half dozen aerial robots prepared to defend him should it be necessary.

He studied the man who had spoken. Short, thick of body and mind, he did not impress Cameron unduly. Cameron decided before the man said another word that he was little more than an errand boy, a human messenger in a world where that function was better served by robots.

"What is it? Has Dr. Suarez come out of his hibernation?"

"Suarez?" The man frowned, as if the name meant nothing to him. Cameron watched as slow recognition came. "Oh, no. I don't work for him. I'm what you might call freelance."

"With an emphasis on free," Cameron said. Nothing about this man seemed professional. A report came from the aerial robot coordinating recon on the man. For all his blocky body and slow wits, he sported enough armament to fight a moderately sized war. Cameron noted with some satisfaction that the coordination robot had adequately evaluated the situation and had signalled for a dozen more mechanical killers.

"You are the Cameron from Gamma Tertius 4? You work for Interstellar Materials?"

"I'm on . . . vacation. Paradise is lovely."

"Yeah, well, I got some information you might want to look at."

The man held out a small photo of Barton Kinsolving. Cameron did his best to conceal his interest.

"What of him?" Cameron asked.

"I killed him."

Cameron did not know if he should rejoice or simply strangle the man for robbing him of his revenge.

CHAPTER SIX

"YOU LOOK LIKE DEATH just walked in and tapped you on the shoulder, Bart, darling." Lark Versalles stretched like an Earthly jungle cat and relaxed. She lay completely naked on the soft couch and knew the effect her movement had on him. More and more, she had begun teasing him, taunting him to provoke a response.

Kinsolving didn't like it. And he was beginning not to like Lark very much. They had been on-planet for over a week and all she wanted to do was explore the ever-changing array of perversions Paradise offered its guests. He had tried to convince her of the need to discover who had tried to kill him aboard Almost Paradise. She had been more than uninterested—she had been openly hostile. Lark had not called him a liar, but the word had all too often danced on her lips without actually being spoken.

"Enjoy all this. You're not paying for it. Daddy is, and he probably has no idea what it costs—or ever will." A hint of bitterness crept into her voice whenever Lark mentioned her parents.

"We've got to do more," protested Kinsolving. He paced as if he had been placed in a zoo cage. As he walked to and fro, he surveyed the "cage." Few animals had ever been given such noble treatment. On Earth he had seen pictures of the ultrarich's homes. This put all those to shame. Opulence on this scale had been reserved for only a privileged few in all history. And here he, a mining engineer and fugitive, was given the run of a modern castle.

All he needed to do was ask and an obedient servant would obey. Robots, humans, the entire mansion overflowed with them. Never did they intrude, but always they hovered just outside his line of sight.

"This is a nice place," Lark said, lolling back. Her legs drifted open slightly in invitation to him. The swirls of cosmetic dye on face and shoulders, however, told him that she was not interested in sex at the moment. He had no idea what did interest her.

"Nice?" he cried. "It's almost criminal to live like this."

"There's nothing criminal. GPMT is paying for it and the company earned the money honestly. Or as honestly as any company ever could. They sell drugs that heal and ease pain and make life longer and better. Why shouldn't we both enjoy the result of that?"

Kinsolving had no good answer for her. He had been unable to find who had tried to kill him. No way off Paradise existed until repairs were finished on the *von Neumann*. The damages had been more extensive than he had thought; the head of maintenance said it might be another week before the yacht was spaceworthy again. At first Kinsolving had thought this was only a ploy to entice Lark to spend more money—more of her father's money. Then he realized that the waiting list for even a day's stay on Paradise was impossibly long. They had no need to bilk GPMT or Lark or anyone.

Even more galling than his inability to board the starship and leave to seek out those who might help him fight the Stellar Death Plan was his repeated failure to see any of those aliens on Paradise gathered for their trade conference. The Trekan ambassador might as well have been the forty parsecs back on his home world. Sensors ringed his huge estate and prevented anyone from entering. Kinsolving had scouted the perimeter and had found how thorough those on Paradise were in granting a guest's wish for privacy.

The most humiliating part had been a TR agent taking him aside after being stopped from sneaking into the alien diplomat's compound and offering a mock infiltration. The agent had guaranteed that Kinsolving would not know the difference between an actor and the real ambassador, that the guards would be good—if this playacting happened to be Kinsolving's most heartfelt fantasy.

"Lark," he said earnestly, sitting on the edge of the sofa. Kinsolving tried to ignore the bare foot that the woman ran up and down his thigh. "The Stellar Death Plan has not been halted because we don't see any evidence of it. I need to tell someone else about it. The more who know, the less likely Hamilton Fremont and the others will be able to carry out their genocide."

The look of extreme boredom on her face carried over to the colors beneath the skin. The cosmetic dyes turned darker, more ominous. Kinsolving thought that storm clouds gathered around her finely boned, lovely face.

Then the sun came out from behind the clouds and Lark smiled brightly. But it was nothing he had done or said.

"Sheeda!" the woman cried. "Come on in. Where have you been, you naughty girl?"

Sheeda moved with catlike grace and slipped between Kinsolving and Lark on the sofa, her body pressing warmly against Kinsolving's. He tried to move away. A strong arm circled his shoulders and held him firmly. No matter how he tried, Kinsolving could not push away the revulsion he felt toward the Onarian. Sheeda looked and acted female, but the male genitalia shocked Kinsolving. And this made him even angrier at himself.

"I've been exploring. There are such nice caves not a kilometer away. Wondrous caves. We can explore, the three of us. Grottos opening onto the ocean, caverns with floors covered with moss softer than this carpet." Sheeda almost purred as she ran her bare feet over the luxurious pile rug. "Everywhere you look, a new and better spot for making love. Come, Lark, Barton, let's go now."

"Photonic!" cried Lark. "We can be there before sunset."

"You are such a poet, Lark," said Sheeda. "We can be making love as the sun vanishes into the ocean. Our bodies will turn all the colors of the sunset."

"Come on, Bart, darling," urged Lark. She tugged at his hand. He resisted. "Be like that. Sheeda and I will enjoy ourselves."

Sheeda rose lithely and paused for a moment on tiptoe, caught and frozen like a bug in amber. The look she gave him was one of sorrow. Kinsolving felt shock that Sheeda pitied him. The spell broke and Sheeda spun and dashed off with Lark. He started to call to them, to beg to be included. Kinsolving stopped himself and watched until they had vanished on their idyll.

He slumped back, eyes closed and mind spinning. No

matter how he tried to concentrate, Kinsolving got nowhere.

"Might as well be sucked into a black hole for all the good I'm doing," he muttered to himself. A small sound caused him to jerk upright, ready for a fight. A human servant stood a meter away.

"Sir, you are unhappy. Your brainwaves show intense displeasure. If Lark and Sheeda do not interest you, may I suggest another form of amusement?"

"No."

"You have shown some desire to meet alien lifeforms."

"Sheeda's an Onarian," he pointed out.

The servant nodded. Kinsolving wondered how the small man kept his hair in such styled perfection. "That is true, sir," the servant said, "but it is in a sexual fashion that you have rejected her company. We might be able to arrange a social meeting with one of another species, if this is your wish."

Kinsolving shook his head. He knew what this offer meant. An actor, not an alien, would be introduced to him. He needed to forge a bond of trust with an alien in a position of power.

How else could he warn them of the Stellar Death Plan?

"I want to talk to someone in charge," he said.

"I am authorized to take care of any complaint. *Any* complaint," the servant said.

"Never mind." Kinsolving swung out of the room, wanting to run in frustration. But where would he run to? Paradise was a resort. For him, it had become a cell as confining as that of the Lorr prison world. The only difference lay in the quality of life.

Kinsolving slowed his gait and walked into a small commons area a half kilometer from his mansion. Few people sat in the carefully gardened area. Most who came to Paradise had specific ideas of enjoyment in mind—pleasures unavailable anywhere else. Kinsolving had gotten a glimmering of some by watching Lark and Sheeda together. On any other world, such coupling between species would have been considered perverted or a major crime. On Paradise, it was accepted as easily as breathing.

He walked aimlessly, trying to choose a definite course of action. The very luxury around him took some of the edge off his determination. Was mass species extinction so important? Let the aliens look after themselves. After all, much of what Fremont and the others said was true. The alien worlds locked together in an alliance against Earth.

Kinsolving heaved a deep sigh. The aliens did exclude humans in trade, in scientific exchange, in most fields. And it was for a good reason. Kinsolving knew humans. Pushy, aggressive to the point of recklessness, Earth had burst forth on the universe thinking to seize and conquer it as it already had a tiny solar system. The aliens had been starfaring for centuries or even millennia. No race welcomed competition, especially from those they considered immature.

He did not blame them. But they ought to be warned of the dangers facing them. Even a spoiled child can turn vicious and do great harm.

A buzzing caused Kinsolving to stop. He cocked his head to one side, listening intently. The sound was all too familiar. He tried to believe that none of IM's brain burners had found their way to Paradise, but he had to admit that such an addictive device would be popular here. Kinsolving followed the humming to a small niche carved in a head-high hedge awash in a tide of red and green blossoms.

He did not recognize the species of alien crouched in the small square formed by the hedge. Kinsolving did recognize the brain burner. The alien's eyes had glazed over and all rigidity had left his body. He slumped to one side, twitching feebly. Kinsolving dropped to his knees and tried to examine the creature.

The pebbly gray skin proved dry and warm. The irises had turned into ovals of gently changing color. Respiration was minimal. Kinsolving had no idea which, if any, of the conditions were abnormal.

"Medic!" he called. "Medical alert. Home in on my voice."

"Sir," came the almost immediate response from a small robot hovering at waist level. "This being is in no immediate danger of expiring."

"The brain burner. What condition is his mind?"

"Damaged."

"Do something. Help him."

"Sir, orders on this point are strict. He has requested no aid should he be found in this condition."

"Take me to your supervisor. Your *human* supervisor."

"At once." The robot's limited decision-making circuits had worked through the problems and chosen a course of least interference. Allowing Kinsolving to badger a human removed him as an annoyance and possible disruptive element in the alien's fantasy/addiction.

Kinsolving followed the robot along a crazy course through the commons area, down a small paved path, up steps and into a tiny garden that looked like something that had been transplanted from Earth. On Paradise, its simplicity was strikingly out of place.

"Who—" began Kinsolving. The robot guiding him had vanished.

He shrugged this off and touched the door panel. The annunciator chimed deep inside the house. Several minutes passed before a harassed looking woman came to the door. Seeing a human instead of a robot startled Kinsolving.

"I'm sorry. A robot brought me here. By mistake, it appears."

"You're Mr. Kinsolving."

"You know me?" He studied the woman more carefully. Ten centimeters shorter than his own one-eighty and considerably more fragile in appearance, she might have been just another guest except for a few details which did not fit. She was not dressed—or undressed—in the fashion of the guests on Paradise. The auburn-haired woman wore a simple dress out of fashion a dozen years ago on Earth.

The idea of this being some rich woman's fantasy vanished when he stared into her brown eyes. Kinsolving almost took a step back. Intensity and intelligence shone forth in an almost dazzling display.

"My name is Vandy Azmotega." She held out a thin hand for him to shake.

"I'm sorry. Am I supposed to know you?"

"Come in, Mr. Kinsolving, and let's talk for a few minutes." He did not miss the small eye motion toward an analog chronometer mounted on the wall. Vandy Azmotega's life ran according to a strict timetable and he had just been granted precious seconds of it.

The decor matched the exterior of the house. Simple, unpretentious, an oasis of taste in an overdecorated world.

"You seem to like my humble house," Vandy said, a small smile crinkling her lips.

"Better than most of the places you rent out." He sat down in a comfortable chair and for the first time in weeks managed to relax. The setting did not demand reaction from him, as did the spacious, awe-inspiring mansion he shared with Lark and Sheeda.

"The robot told me you had come upon . . . a guest."

"He was burning out his brain with a device manufactured by Interstellar Materials," Kinsolving said bluntly. "IM lets the aliens get addicted to lower power brain burners, then starts distributing high intensity units. By that time, the alien is so addicted to the private paradise granted by the device he is unable to stop. He ends up a drooling husk."

"You are quite frank, Mr. Kinsolving. This surprises me."

"That IM is doing it? They are doing it on many worlds. Zeta Orgo 4. Contact a law enforcement officer there named Quixx for full details."

Vandy perched on the edge of a chair, arms crossed on her chest, watching him like a hunting bird watches its prey. "Because of their capacity for inflicting permanent damage, I've tried to stem the tide of the devices—the brain burners, as you called them—and have failed. In a way, it is not my responsibility. TR makes it very clear that Paradise exists for *any* recreation." Vandy Azmotega made a wry face. "You would be startled at what passes for recreation among some species."

"I doubt it." Kinsolving paused, then asked, "You're the supervisor on Paradise, aren't you?"

"Although I don't advertise my position, neither do I make it a secret."

"I'm surprised that the supervisor of an entire planetary resort would choose such . . . plain quarters."

"What would your choice be, Mr. Kinsolving? This or where you and your companions are staying?"

"The point is well taken."

"Not many would agree with me, though," Vandy said. She slid back into the chair. She hiked her feet up onto a low wood table and leaned back farther. "Running Paradise is a full-time job," she said. "I like to be surrounded by familiar, comfortable things."

"You do a good job. I don't see anyone complaining."

"Except yourself, Mr. Kinsolving. What can TR do for you that it hasn't?"

Kinsolving liked Vandy Azmotega, but she was obviously highly placed in Terra Recreations' power structure. No one gained sole dominion over an entire world, especially one as profitable as Paradise, without being highly competent and even more highly thought of in corporate circles.

"You mentioned the influx of brain burners," he said, skirting the question. "You don't approve but TR does?"

"Something like that. There are other kinds of drugs and devices used that I am not pleased with allowing on-planet, but . . ." She shrugged her shoulders. "I am not appointed dictator of morality. All my company expects of me is that Paradise turn a profit and that the guests enjoy themselves. Why aren't you helping me do my job, Mr. Kinsolving?"

"Bart," he said. "Call me Bart."

"What does it matter? You're not going to enjoy yourself any more if I call you Barton or Mr. Kinsolving."

"Your records must be very good," he observed.

"The best."

"But not complete. I stopped IM on Zeta Orgo 4. When I saw the brain burner, I knew I had to stop them on Paradise."

"You oppose the use of such devices? That's charitable of you, Bart, but it is not your business. If you fancy yourself a savior, we can generate a small scenario for you. You can stop any kind of illicit activity you want. We do complete—"

"No!" he roared. "No fantasies. This is real." Kinsolving found himself telling Vandy of the Stellar Death Plan and how Fremont and the other IM directors wanted to destroy all aliens.

"I am torn between two courses of action," she said after he had finished.

"What?"

"I know you're telling the truth. The probes that have been focused on you show basal metabolic rates, galvanic skin responses, eye dilations, perspiration levels, a dozen other indicators. You are telling the truth as you know it."

"As I know it? It's true!"

"You *think* it's true. That can mean one of three things. You might be entirely crazy, in which case you would believe everything you say no matter how far out in orbit. Another possibility is that what you say is the truth, but that you are wrong. You might be the victim of some elaborate joke. Your co-workers, perhaps."

"That's ridiculous."

"I think so, too. The final possibility is that what you relate has actually happened."

"It comes down to answers one or three, is that it?"

"Crazy as a quark or the discoverer of a fiendish plot," she said, nodding.

Kinsolving calmed a little. "Which is it?"

Vandy did not answer. She continued to study him. But Kinsolving saw subtle changes in her expression.

"You believe me," he said. "Why?"

"I've reported incidents similar to the alien with the illegal brain burner to my superiors. They have done nothing. Recently, I have been ordered to accommodate certain researchers from the TR home office. I have not been allowed to examine the laboratories nor have I been told what research is being conducted. This is both unusual and offensive. I ought to be in complete charge of the planet. My immediate superior has refused to give a satisfactory explanation of the company's motives."

"You think it is something illegal?"

"More than that. Several alien guests have died. I cannot connect the arrival of Suarez—Morgan Suarez, the chief of research—but it is suspicious. Before his arrival, no deaths of any species. After he has been here a few months, four deaths."

"When was the last?"

"This afternoon," she said, frowning. "That one was a murder. A killer robot, is the best diagnosis from my med staff."

"A killer robot?" Kinsolving felt a chill of premonition pass along his spine. Cameron might not be dead, but how could the robot master ever have discovered him on Paradise? Kinsolving had not known his destination when leaving the Zeta Orgo system. He had taken the first alignment in an attempt to evade the Lorr.

"You make that sound as if you know more than I do," Vandy said.

"Has anyone named Cameron arrived? An IM official?"

"No to both questions."

"Sandy hair, steel gray eyes, medium height, stocky."

"Mr. Kinsolving—Barton—that might describe a hundred humans on Paradise. And more than a few aliens, too."

"I have no idea how far-reaching the Plan is among top level executives. It seems incredible to me that others beside Fremont might be involved, but it's possible."

"You aren't implying that Terra Recreations is involved in planetary genocide?"

"Perhaps not TR any more than the vast majority of IM. What of a few key officers?"

"Too far off orbit for my liking."

"What if only Suarez and his—your—superior are involved?" Kinsolving saw that the woman could accept this.

"Those two always were the little lost nebulas in TR," she said, thinking aloud. "They glowed and puffed and no one noticed them. With egos like theirs, that must be intolerable."

"Can we examine Suarez's lab? Without him knowing it?" He saw a peculiar expression on her face. "You've tried to get your surveillance vidcams in, haven't you?"

"I have," she admitted. "No use. I gave up. Running Paradise is a job requiring utmost attention to detail. Suarez is authorized to be here and to act independent of my staff." She shrugged, as if saying this ended her involvement. Kinsolving saw that her interest went much deeper.

"There are ways of observing without using robots," he said.

"Break into Suarez's lab? I cannot condone criminal activity on Paradise."

"It wouldn't be criminal if the planetary supervisor inspected equipment under her control, would it?"

"What are we looking for?" Vandy asked.

To that Kinsolving had no idea. But he had the gut level feeling that it might be more insidious than the brain burners. Even worse, he had the feeling that Cameron was involved.

Vandy Azmotega stood and gestured to Kinsolving. "Let's go do some burgling," she said. A slow smile crossed her face until she positively beamed. "What a fantasy this is! I've always wanted to be a desperate character, breaking into places and stealing things."

"Why didn't you arrange for a week or two of recreational fantasy?" Kinsolving asked.

"Wouldn't be the same. I'd know the difference. That's one of the penalties for spending all my time manufacturing fantasies for other people. You learn the difference. Reality can't be improved on, is my motto."

Kinsolving understood. And he would know the difference between a harmless experiment in Suarez's lab and one connected with the Stellar Death Plan.

CHAPTER SEVEN

CAMERON TOOK THE PHOTO from the man's hand and peered at it. "How did you kill him?" he asked in a mild voice that carried an edge of chilled steel.

"Shoved him down a waste disposal chute up on Almost Paradise."

"The space station," mused Cameron. His quick mind worked over possibilities and he did not like the answers he came to. The only reason Kinsolving would have chosen Paradise as a destination after fleeing Zeta Orgo was knowledge of the project Dr. Suarez undertook. How such information could have leaked out—and to Kinsolving, embroiled as he was with the unpleasantness with the arachnoid Bizzies on Web—eluded Cameron.

A significant security breach. Nothing else made sense. It lay beyond the realm of chance that Kinsolving had picked this planet at random when he fled.

Still, a muscle in Cameron's cheek twitched when he thought of Barton Kinsolving. Every trap he had laid for the former mining engineer had failed. Kinsolving had entered the secret offices IM used to carry out their part in the Plan—and had escaped. Kinsolving had escaped a phalanx of superbly wrought robots on Web. Had Kinsolving stumbled onto Suarez? Impossible, thought Cameron. Yet...

A tiny buzz from the automedic warned Cameron that his blood pressure was rising. He forced himself to relax.

"You know me?" he asked of the shorter man. "How do you know of my interest in this one?" He tapped Kinsolving's photo.

"You don't belong to TR," the man said. "I do. You and I are in the same line of work."

"That hardly seems likely."

"Name's Davi Jessarette." Cameron ignored the outthrust hand. Jessarette lowered it, a perplexed look on his face. "We got similar interests."

"In Kinsolving?"

"If that's his real name. I got this photo some time back from headquarters. Rumors came with it that you were hot to get rid of him. Everybody's heard of you, Cameron. Everybody."

Cameron seethed. This fool had no idea who he had tried to murder—to hear Jessarette tell it, *had* murdered. Cameron could not discount the chance that Jessarette had succeeded where he had failed so often, but nothing about the man inspired confidence.

"I want to examine the body," Cameron said.

Jessarette smiled. Two of his teeth had been broken and improperly fixed. Cameron edged away and unconsciously smoothed wrinkles from his own impeccably styled and fashionable clothing. The plum-colored doublet matched well with the burnt umber, skintight silk breeches with the silver conches. The flowing sleeves with their fluted ridges concealed enough electronics equipment to destroy half the planet; Cameron took pride in knowing that none of it showed.

Certainly not like this fool's heavy armaments. Not only did he have faulty teeth, his tailor had done nothing to insure that the lines of his clothing would remain unmarred by the sundry pistols and grenades he so obviously carried.

Cameron fleetingly considered bringing down a few robots and seeing how Jessarette handled them. If they killed him, no loss. If he lived, Cameron might better believe the tall tale of him slaying Kinsolving.

"No way," said Jessarette, grinning even wider. Cameron found himself unable to look away from the bad dental work. It repulsed him even as he stared at it. "I shoved his body into a disposal unit. It kicked him out of the station under pressure. His body burned up in Paradise's atmosphere. A clean kill."

"What were the events leading up to Kinsolving's ... demise?"

"Saw him trying to talk to the Trekan ambassador. I got orders to let nobody near the Bizzie. I recognized him from the photo, slugged him and shoved his carcass into the disposal."

"Quaint."

"Effective," Jessarette said with some pride.

"Why do you think that you and I share the same profession?"

"You're from Interstellar Materials' Security Directorate. I saw the records. You came to observe the test Suarez is going to run. The doc uses such weird metals in his lab, it makes sense that IM is supplying them."

"I know of no such 'weird metals,'" Cameron said truthfully. He had no interest in Morgan Suarez's work other than carrying out Villalobos' orders to observe. It came as no surprise, however, that IM supplied the scientist with rare metals, possibly some of the rare earths mined on Deepdig where Kinsolving had been supervisor.

Cameron seized on this thread. Had Kinsolving learned of this project some time ago? Now that he had ruined IM's planned distribution of brain burners on Zeta Orgo 4, did he turn his attention to other uncovered Plan projects?

Again the automedic warned him. He could not keep calm thinking of Kinsolving's interference in the Plan. Cameron reached up and toggled off the warning device.

"You on drugs?" asked Jessarette. "Never saw anyone wearing one of those who didn't get regular jolts."

"You learned of my presence from Suarez's records?"

"Space, don't get all nuked off over this. Suarez might not have known I was reading everything. He gets careless with records sometimes."

Cameron filed this away for future use. A researcher working for the Plan should never become careless. If an inept minor security officer like Jessarette could successfully spy, someone as clever as Kinsolving could learn everything about the project in a few minutes. Hadn't Kinsolving penetrated IM headquarters, found the secret offices used by Liu and the others and learned enough to prevent the deaths of more than four billion Bizarres?

Damn Kinsolving!

He took a deep breath. No matter what Jessarette said, Cameron did not believe Kinsolving had died. He had to proceed on the basis that the man still lived and still actively worked against the Plan.

"Perhaps we might exchange... techniques," Cameron said, hiding his loathing. "After all, as you said, we are in the same line of work."

"Photonic!" Jessarette exclaimed. "Want to go and split

a bottle? They got some good Earth whiskey at the employee commissary."

"Let's return to my bungalow. More private."

"Right. No snoops listening in. I heard how good you are with the robots." Davi Jessarette looked around, as if he might visually spot them. Cameron checked his small robot patrol. No one listened to their conversation or had them under electronic surveillance. He had no way to tell if someone at a distance watched them through an optical device, though this seemed a remote possibility. It never paid to take chances. He had been careless just once and Kinsolving had sent him to the hospital with serious brain injury.

The pair of assassins walked slowly back to Cameron's bungalow. Cameron silently motioned Jessarette to enter, noting that the man took no precautions. A trap might have been laid. He did nothing to check for even simple surveillance probes.

Cameron punched a drink order into the drink computer and waited for the glasses to rise from the countertop.

"How come you don't have full vocal command?" asked Jessarette.

Cameron shrugged to cover the shudder of disgust he felt for this ignorant fool. "A quirk. I prefer to do things myself."

"Weird," said Jessarette, taking the drink offered him by Cameron. "But the stories I heard about you say you're top of the line. None better."

"How did you get into this line of work? Are you employed by TR's home office or by the planetary supervisor?" Cameron settled into a straight-backed chair and waited for the drug he had placed in Jessarette's drink to take effect. A small robot hovering unnoticed a few centimeters behind Jessarette's head monitored the drug's progress through the man's bloodstream. When it winked green Cameron knew that the drug had effectively paralyzed this clumsy assassin.

"I got into it by accident," Jessarette said. The expression on his face told of the conflict raging within. He wanted to lie, to make his cold-blooded murdering seem more glamorous. Cameron cared little for this. He wanted information and complete obedience from Jessarette.

"Tell me about Kinsolving. Was there any reason other than the one you've mentioned for you to attempt to kill him?"

"No. I... I hadn't killed anyone in a long time. I needed the feel. The photo came through Bizzie channels with a flag on it from the home office about him."

Cameron closed his eyes and rubbed his forehead. He murdered without qualm. He had done so many times. The exact numbers dead because of his robotic assassins lay beyond reckoning, but never had he experienced a thrill from the act. He worked for Maria Villalobos, for Interstellar Materials, for his own ends. The Stellar Death Plan fit well into his personal view of the universe. The Bizzies had to be stopped and Earth governments were failing miserably in accomplishing that end.

But to kill for the stark enjoyment of it was as alien to him as any Bizarre. His opinion of Davi Jessarette dropped even lower.

"Do you know for a fact that Kinsolving's body was evacuated through the disposal? Did you watch?"

"No." The word twisted Jessarette's lips. He tried to lie and could not. Cameron's drug worked very well. He would have to thank his friend at Galaxy Pharmaceuticals and Medical Techtronics who had given him a few milliliters of the experimental potion.

"Tell me about Dr. Suarez's work."

"I'm not supposed to."

"You *want* to. More than anything else in the universe."

"It's a plague. He wants to test it on the Bizzies vacationing on Paradise."

"The nature of this plague?" Cameron did not expect an answer, nor did he get one. Such information lay beyond Jessarette's ability to comprehend. "Who knows of this trial?"

"Me. Suarez and his assistants. No one else."

"Not even the planetary supervisor?"

"No. Vandy Azmotega doesn't know about the Plan."

"Stand," ordered Cameron. "Put down your drink. You will show me Suarez's labs. There is no need to inform the doctor of our visit. We will explore secretly, without allowing anyone to see us, until I say otherwise. Do you understand?"

"Yes." Sweat broke out on Jessarette's forehead as he fought the orders. Cameron noted that the battle did not last long. Jessarette's will was far weaker than the mind-controlling drug.

Cameron followed a half dozen paces behind Jessarette. If the man made a mistake and blundered into a defensive system, Cameron wanted him to expire first. A quick glance showed more than a dozen robots floating at different levels, some barely above the ground, others as high as ten meters. Cameron felt secure behind such a formidable defensive screen of robot killers.

"The lab," called Jessarette after they had followed a small gravel path for almost a kilometer.

Cameron motioned. An aerial robot shot forward and returned almost instantly. He inserted a decoder into his ear to receive the robot's encoded surveillance report. A short burst carried full information about the laboratory. Only a few inconsequential sensors dotted the area. Cameron saw why Jessarette had been able to enter and spy so easily. Suarez desperately needed a competent security agent to protect this project.

"Disable the sensors," Cameron ordered two robots. Less than a minute passed before he received microburst assurance from the robots that the task had been satisfactorily completed.

How efficient they were compared to the doltish Jessarette!

"Inside," Cameron ordered his drugged guide. "Show me the records office where you learned so much about the Plan."

Jessarette entered the door. Cameron cast a quick look around, not really expecting to see anyone. The robots had given the clear signal on the corridors and office. He followed Jessarette into the small office and pushed the man aside. Sitting in front of the computer console, Cameron began work.

He did not like what he saw. Too much sensitive material had been entered into the computer data banks without adequate protection. It had taken him only a few tries to find the key. Even with his expertise, he should have needed a day or longer to break the codes. What bothered him the most was the easy availability to anyone simply blundering into the office. They need not be looking specifically for information. All they needed to do was glance at the unprotected screen and learn more than had been revealed by all the other adherents to the Plan since its inception four years earlier.

Cameron watched the slow march of information about Project Unravel. He speeded up the readout and let a robot record the full information. He could study it in detail later. When information about the security measures and personnel came on-screen, his full attention returned.

Complete personnel dossiers on the project scientists amplified what he had been told by Villalobos. Very little about Jessarette showed. A few entries about Vandy Azmotega confirmed Jessarette's appraisal that she knew nothing about the Plan.

"Enough," Cameron said, leaning back in the chair. "I know enough about Project Unravel to take command."

"Command? But Dr. Suarez has full authority from TR headquarters. He reports directly to the director of off-planet operations," said Jessarette.

"It is interesting to note that the chairman of TR's board is not involved in the Plan," said Cameron, more to himself than to Jessarette.

"Dr. Suarez is in charge."

"No," Cameron said in a velvet voice. "I am the new leader of the project. You will obey me in all matters. Your superiors want this. Do you understand?"

Jessarette's willpower had faded to nothing under the drug's influence. He nodded eagerly.

"Take me to Morgan Suarez. We have much to discuss, the doctor and I." Cameron followed his drugged cohort from the office, more confident than he had been since leaving the hospital on Gamma Tertius 4. Under his guidance, Project Unravel could kill billions of Bizzies.

The Stellar Death Plan would be served. And Cameron would seize the IM directorship that should have been his!

CHAPTER EIGHT

"THIS DOESN'T LOOK like much," Barton Kinsolving said. He peered around a large-boled tree at the research facility. The small building stood a mere one story tall and could not contain more than five moderately sized rooms. "Suarez must not have much equipment."

"He has almost four metric tons," came Vandy Azmotega's answer. She pressed close to Kinsolving, spying on the lab as if she had never seen it before. Kinsolving understood her excitement. The woman supervised the fantasies of others and never indulged herself. This small personal surveillance excursion gave her the opportunity to sample what the guests accepted as their due.

Kinsolving had worried about trusting Vandy until he saw the sparkle in her eyes as they skirted the perimeter of Suarez's laboratory. She would not have been so excited if she had known what went on inside. Kinsolving had given her an excuse to find out, and Vandy Azmotega was stimulated by it. Only a superb actress could fake her reaction.

"He must be crowded—or it must be as massive as neutronium."

"A large portion of this complex is underground. We used it as storage before Dr. Suarez arrived. There are service tunnels leading to some of the rooms."

"Never show the guest how the magic is performed, is that it?" he asked.

"Exactly. No one wants a vacation spoiled by listening to loader robots clanking around above ground."

"Sensors?"

"Only a couple warning devices put there to keep away curious guests. I don't know if Suarez has added more. I haven't checked on him. Being ordered to leave him alone helped, too. There's too much to attend to on Paradise without adding a researcher."

Kinsolving dropped to the ground and wriggled forward

on his belly. The first sensor he found had been deactivated. He examined it carefully and saw the pockmarks of small laser burns on its case. Someone had already entered —and had not wanted to announce himself.

"Burned out," he said. "Unless I miss my guess, all the sensors are burned out."

"I'll have to alert the repair crews. They don't usually slack off like this."

Kinsolving swallowed hard. He knew that telepathic powers were a fantasy, that action at a distance was not possible. But he had the crawling sensation up and down his spine that he knew who had preceded them. For several days he had the hunch—the precognition—that Cameron was here. Such sensor destruction, done with efficiency and skill, carried Cameron's trademark.

"What's wrong, Bart?" asked Vandy. "You look as if you stabbed yourself."

"Your repair crews aren't falling behind in their work. The sensors aren't even putting out 'damaged' signals."

"But they..."

"Cameron's work. I'm sure of it."

"The man you asked about?"

"He must be here. I'd hoped he had died on Zeta Orgo, but I didn't know for sure."

"He followed you?"

To that Kinsolving had no answer. It sounded paranoid for him to agree, yet it seemed too much of a coincidence for Cameron to come to Paradise to take part in Suarez's project. From what Vandy had said, Suarez was a biologist, not a roboticist. Did the experiment, whatever it was, require Cameron's expertise? Kinsolving knew that there was only one way to find out.

"Let's see what is going on inside. Will the researchers be in the underground section?"

Vandy shrugged. "Probably. Dr. Suarez hasn't seen fit to confide in me." Something in her tone alerted Kinsolving.

"Is that unusual?"

"Not really. We have HPGs—highly placed guests—on Paradise all the time, usually top officials from Terra Recreations. Some are secretive, but not like Suarez. With him, everything came as an order from the vice president in charge of off-world resorts—my boss."

"And?" Kinsolving urged. "What else is bothering you? The aliens' deaths?"

"More than the deaths. Although it's difficult to say, I think that as many as four more aliens are missing."

"Why don't you know? I thought you kept track of all your guests."

"Some want privacy. I've been told that on some alien worlds, especially those with hivelike societies, it's a perversion to want to be alone."

"You get those aliens."

"On Paradise it isn't a perversion," Vandy said indignantly. In a lower voice, she added, "Even some of the acts human society has ruled to be pervo are done here. No harm to others, maximum pleasure to our guests. That's our motto."

"Nothing wrong in that," said Kinsolving. But his mind soared ahead. He cared little what happened on Paradise— unless it meant a new plot in the Stellar Death Plan being started. If Cameron had come to Paradise, and if Morgan Suarez was working on a secret project, Kinsolving could only conclude that a new method of genocide was being researched. Luck had come his way in finding a highly placed official of TR not involved with the Plan and concerned with the deaths in her jurisdiction.

He touched Vandy's arm and motioned for her to enter the small building. She started off, walking carefully. Once, she bent over to examine a damaged sensor. Other than this, she made no suspicious movements. Kinsolving's confidence in her grew.

Standing in the doorway, she turned and said, "Empty. They must be at the lower levels."

A tiny flash of light caught Kinsolving's attention. He yelled and dived forward, arms circling Vandy's waist. She cried out in surprise as his weight carried her into the building. His tackle had been perfectly timed; the aerial killer robot flashed by on its deadly trajectory, missing her by millimeters.

"Robot," he panted out in explanation, rolling over and trying to get free. He yelped in pain as the robot spun on its axis and fired a small laser. The beam burned away part of his sleeve and bit deeply into his triceps.

"It fired a laser!" Vandy Azmotega sounded stunned that such a minuscule aerial device could carry a deadly weapon.

"Get out of here," Kinsolving ordered. He jerked her hard against a wall. The laser cut a deep groove in the hardwood floor, leaving behind a smoldering cut almost a centimeter deep. "It might not follow you."

Vandy scrambled to her feet and ducked outside the building. Kinsolving had ripped off his shirt by this time. He jumped to one side, avoiding the deadly lance of coherent light. In the same motion, he cast his shirt like a net.

The robot burned a hole through it with a single microsecond burst. But Kinsolving had achieved his purpose. The visual sensors on the sides of the slender robot were momentarily blocked. He grabbed for it and jerked around, smashing it to the floor. Kinsolving felt metal and boron composite yield. He also felt a new explosion of pain in his hand and leg. The laser beam had shot through his calf and left palm.

Beyond conscious thought, he stamped hard on the crippled robot. A new pain, this time in his heel. Then came the satisfying crunch of metal. He had crushed the killer robot.

"Barton, you're hurt. All over!"

"I'll be fine. It's dead."

"Deactivated," she corrected. "Robots aren't alive."

"This one might as well have been. Clever, quick, tiny, smarter than most human assassins."

"So small," she agreed. "Hardly longer than my little finger. How could it carry such a powerful weapon?"

"This is Cameron's handiwork. I'm sure of it." He pulled Vandy from the building. "He set the robot to protect his back. It probably signalled intrusion the instant it fired the first laser bolt."

"You make it sound intelligent. There's no way to put even the most rudimentary intelligence into such a small machine."

"Cameron does it all the time. The man's a robotics genius." He kept pulling her along until they had gone several hundred meters into a thicket. Kinsolving didn't know if this would be far enough to discourage pursuit by other robot sentries. He hoped so. They showed true intelligence and might reason that following Kinsolving could be a diversion. Kinsolving waited several minutes, every sense alert, but no new robots appeared.

"That wasn't one of the approved TR sensors," Vandy said. She looked at him, brown eyes wide. "This mythical Cameron," she said. "He works for IM?"

Kinsolving nodded. He tore away the burned cloth around his leg wounds. The searing beam had cauterized as it passed through. The burn on his left palm proved more painful than disabling. Even the one through his heel did not slow him—much. He slipped back into his shirt. The beam had burned through a spot directly over his heart; he was glad he had not been wearing it when the robot killer had fired.

"We've got to see what they're doing," Vandy said with real determination. "I refuse to allow this to go on in Paradise. Dammit, this is *my* world, my responsibility." Cameron stopped her before she could storm off.

"Where do you think you're going?"

"To alert security."

"How loyal are they—to you personally?"

"No," she said, shocked at what he implied. Vandy Azmotega was even more shocked when he told her in detail what had happened to him aboard Almost Paradise.

"It might have been a TR security officer," Kinsolving finished.

She shook her head but no words formed. He let her consider the possibility that she no longer controlled Paradise, then asked, "Where are the entrances to the underground service tunnels? We can enter the lab that way."

"There's an entrance over there somewhere." She pointed to a camouflaged grate set flush with the ground. Kinsolving brushed dirt and leaves away from the lock. Vandy reached past, using a card key to open the grate. It slid silently into its frame, a small light coming on to light a metal rung ladder.

"Go back to your office and get guards you can trust," he said, swinging down to get his feet on the ladder. "And don't include the ones who were on Almost Paradise—especially any guarding the Trekan ambassador."

"Brake back," she snapped. "You're missing orbit by a solar system. I'm not letting you go down there alone. I know the tunnels and you don't." She looked at him sheepishly. "And I don't think I can trust *any* of my security personnel. Not after what you just told me."

Kinsolving said nothing. Vandy seemed open and honest; her response was what he would expect from someone who doubted—just a little—not only his story but also her own personnel. From much of what she had hinted at, Paradise had become something less in the past few months and this worried her greatly.

"It might be dangerous down there," she said, eyeing the lighted opening with no enthusiasm. "I might be able to come back with a few robot workers. We could send them ahead to see if it's safe."

"No," Kinsolving said. "That would only warn Suarez and Cameron, unless your robots usually patrol the tunnels."

"Not here," she said, shaking her head. Her auburn hair had become slightly matted with sweat. Kinsolving saw the strain working on the woman. She had been entrusted with the safety and security of guests on Paradise. All that had slipped away gradually. Confronting the source of her problem lay beyond her training. Even though Kinsolving had no reason to believe it, he doubted if she had experienced anything more deadly than not having enough intoxicants for her customers.

Kinsolving took a deep breath, then swung around and started down the ladder. The rungs cut at his hands; it had been many months since any human had ventured here. At the bottom he peered along a tunnel so dark that he would have to feel his way. For him, it was almost like coming home. He missed the mine shafts. Being an engineer had taken him deep beneath planetary surfaces enough to enjoy it—or had he always liked the closed-in feeling that drove some people phobic?

"To the left," he said, a sureness in his voice that he did not feel inside.

"That's the way to the lower level in the lab," Vandy said, a tone of surprise in her voice. "You haven't been here before, have you?"

"No." As they walked along the dark tunnel, Kinsolving gingerly feeling his way, he told her of his job and life in the mines. Part of him enjoyed holding the woman's hand and talking with her, but another part screamed *danger!* Darkness masked much. Cameron's killer robots could work easily with IR or radar. And there would be no place to fight or run in such a small tunnel. Less than a dozen paces into the tunnel, the lights slowly rose to a level where he could see.

He glanced at Vandy. "Automatic," she said. "Humans trigger the sensors; robots don't."

Kinsolving doubted they would face another human. He worried about Cameron's robots on guard. Even though he watched carefully, he found no sensors, no traps, nothing. This was nothing more than what Vandy claimed: a service tunnel.

"There," she said, seeing the recessed door a few seconds before he did. "That leads into Suarez's lab. I . . . I don't know if he even uses this part of the basement. All I ever used it for was a storeroom."

Kinsolving ran his fingers around the seal on the door. Parts of the silicon rubber seal had dried over the years. He found no indication of tampering for a long, long time. But what really lay on the other side?

He tugged at the door, then had to put a foot against the wall and pull with all his might. When the door yielded, it sent him stumbling back into Vandy. Her arms circled him and they went down in a heap.

"There are easier ways of getting together," she said, laughing. "Not that I mind, but this is hardly the time or place."

"Later?" he asked. For a few brief seconds something other than the Stellar Death Plan and Cameron's mechanical minions entered his mind.

"If there is a later," Vandy said, struggling to get out from under him. Kinsolving got to his feet and helped her up. They peered through the door. Kinsolving had not expected to find anyone—or anything—waiting. The commotion getting the portal open would have drawn instant fire if guards had been posted. A heavy blanket of dust lay over the few crates strewn around. He doubted anyone had been inside this room in more than a year.

He made his way to an inner door. This one he did not immediately open. Sounds from the other side caused him to motion Vandy to silence. She pressed her ear beside his against the plastic panel. Their faces were just a few centimeters apart.

". . . release soon for a field test."

"The lab results do look promising, Dr. Suarez," came another voice.

"Suarez and his assistant," Vandy whispered.

Kinsolving opened the door enough to peer around the edge. The bright light momentarily blinded him and the sharp, astringent smell of a bio lab caused his nose to wrinkle and eyes to water. He waited impatiently and caught a glimpse of Morgan Suarez. The man was small, darkly complected and had jet black hair swept straight back in a severe style that gave him a fanatical aspect.

When Suarez spun suddenly, his hand reaching inside his white lab coat, Kinsolving's heart jumped into his throat. He thought he had been seen. When Suarez drew out a tiny laser, Kinsolving knew the scientist had discovered him.

But Suarez faced off at an angle, his right shoulder to the door. Kinsolving tried to hold Vandy back but the woman pushed around to a spot under him to watch, too.

"What in the empty hell are you doing here?" Suarez demanded. Kinsolving could not see the intruder who upset the biologist but the answering voice was all too familiar.

"You neglect me terribly, doctor," came Cameron's voice. "I do not like to be ignored."

"You overstep your bounds, Cameron. And you, Jessarette, you shouldn't have brought him down here. It's dangerous."

"Jessarette?" Vandy stirred. "He's on the staff as a security specialist. I had him guarding the Trekan ambassador on Almost Paradise. He's supposed to be overseeing security for their conference, not—"

Kinsolving clamped his hand over the woman's mouth. A gaudily dressed man swaggered into view. The bright colors and the soft rustle of natural silks betrayed Cameron as surely as the glints off his guardian robots hovering high in the room. Kinsolving dared not close the door. Such a slight move would alert the robotic killers.

"Mr. Jessarette did not lead me here of his own free will. Let us say that I persuaded him."

Suarez examined Jessarette, who stood docilely. "Drugged," the researcher said. "It might be a derivative from the Astkonian night juggler flower."

"A synthetic," Cameron said, smiling. "You are very knowledgeable. Not many have heard of the night juggler's lovely black flower."

"It only blooms every four planetary rotations—a dozen standard years," snapped Suarez. "What is it you want, Cameron? To discuss botany?"

"To discuss your project. Director Villalobos sent me to oversee progress. You have refused to see me. That is a clear violation of the agreement of friendly cooperation between our superiors."

Vandy Azmotega tried to speak again. Kinsolving tightened his grip. He dared not even hiss at her to be silent. A patrolling robot slowly floated by a meter away. The slender twenty-centimeter-long robot carried enough armament to burn its way clear of a steel-walled vault. Against an unprotected human, it might take only microseconds for a quick kill.

"Project Unravel proceeds well," Suarez said. He moved and returned the impact laser to its hidden holster. Kinsolving did not relax; the robots might be more attentive to other threats.

"Ah, yes, the project. Jessarette has told me something of it. Director Villalobos has gone a bit further. But I need more details, Dr. Suarez. Ones that only you can provide."

"This is a busy time, Cameron." Suarez spun and started off. He stopped and stared. Kinsolving could not see what had halted the scientist, but he thought he knew. In a few seconds a killer robot rose to shoulder level.

"My friends are not likely to allow human emotion to get in the way of a detailed report," Cameron said, obviously enjoying Suarez's discomfort at being confronted with a deadly robot. "A short report, doctor. That is all I ask. At this time."

Cameron moved around. Kinsolving thought the robotics genius lacked some of the swagger he once had in his walk. A hesitancy? Or an injury? Cameron's head wound might have been worse than it appeared. Kinsolving cursed the bad luck that Cameron had not been permanently disabled.

And Kinsolving still wished he had been able to kill Cameron.

"The bioweapon will be introduced soon. The Bizzie conference is a perfect place. There are seven different species attending. Over fourteen hundred aliens total are on-planet, adding a few more species to the count. We shall be able to judge the efficacy of the project by the number who die within a week."

"It unravels their DNA?" asked Cameron.

"Did Jessarette tell you that?" Suarez looked at Davi Jessarette. The look was one of pure contempt.

"I doubt he understands such matters. No, doctor, I unraveled it on my own." Cameron chuckled at the wordplay. "Not everyone you deal with is incompetent—or stupid. Can you imagine, he tried to kill an adversary of mine. I doubt he succeeded. But this is of little consequence. Tell me of Project Unravel."

"You are correct in your appraisal. I have spent almost two years developing a strain of virus that works solely on Bizzie DNA. To humans it is completely harmless."

Vandy stirred again. Kinsolving released his grip but silently cautioned her to remain quiet. She moved back from the door and stood behind him, peering over his shoulder.

"An interesting plague," mused Cameron. "A plague in Paradise."

"I am very busy, Cameron. Get your damned robots out of here and let me work. I'll give you a complete report after the bioweapon is released and analysis is completed."

"No, Dr. Suarez, you'll give it to me now. That was the agreement made by our superiors. Who are we to go against their wishes?"

Suarez made an impatient gesture, then edged around the robot blocking his way. Cameron laughed and followed. Behind him Jessarette walked as if his mind had been burned out. His mouth hung slack and his eyes were dull and unfocused.

"We can't let them do this!" exclaimed Vandy.

Kinsolving started to caution her to silence, then saw it was too late. The robot hovering in the center of the laboratory began to swing about, sensors at full. He closed the door and pushed her across the storeroom to the tunnel beyond.

"Run like the sun's going nova," he told her. "We triggered a guard robot's pursuit sensors."

"But—"

Kinsolving shoved her into the tunnel; she stumbled in the wrong direction. He started to reverse course to head back for the ladder leading to the surface. In the storeroom behind, he heard a sharp hiss. The smell of burned plastic reached his nose. The robot had blasted its way through the door. He closed the door leading from the room into the tunnel, hoping that the robot would scan the entire storeroom before finding it.

He might as well have wished for the device to fuse its own circuits.

Kinsolving pushed hard against Vandy, giving up his hope of reaching the ladder to the surface. "Keep going. It'll be on us in a few seconds. Down there." He jerked her around and sent her reeling down a branching tunnel.

"No, not this way!"

Kinsolving wasn't listening. He herded her in front of him. They ran hard down the long, dimly illuminated corridor. He frantically sought a door, another branching tunnel.

"Barton, no, not that door," she begged. He worked feverishly to pull back locking bars. Kinsolving glanced back down the tunnel. The robot had found their trail. Scent, sound, visual, it no longer mattered how this killer tracked. It had locked onto its target. And it would never stop until they were dead, dead, dead.

Kinsolving ripped open the door and screamed. Rising in front of him was an oyster-white creature fully two meters tall, with enormously powerful arms and savage talons that raked at his face. He ducked and narrowly avoiding having his eyes gouged out. The stench from the beast overwhelmed him. He gagged and dropped to one knee, hands trying vainly to stop the odor.

The furred behemoth turned sluggishly and came for him. Kinsolving sagged back against a wall, all strength gone from his arms and legs. He could only watch as the beast came for its prey—him.

CHAPTER NINE

CAMERON TURNED and frowned when a tiny flash caught his attention. The guard robot he had posted in the corridor had sighted a target and gone after it. The man quickly checked the remaining robots and decided they were adequate to any threat posed by Morgan Suarez and his assistant. He did not bother considering Davi Jessarette in the equation. The night juggler drug still held the clumsy assassin in its thrall.

Suarez saw his sudden inattention and asked, "What's wrong? Did you hear something?"

"Your sensors are inadequate for protecting such a valuable part of the Plan," Cameron said lightly. He wanted to check the prey his robot had locked on but did not want to reveal the full capacity of his defenses to Suarez. Cameron saw that Villalobos had done well to send someone of his ability to oversee the scientist. Although Suarez had the proper instincts for mass destruction and death, he lacked discipline and attention to details. The researcher would be expendable should it become necessary.

Cameron hoped that it would. He needed to hone his talents and test another of his metallic murderers.

"Leave us," Suarez said, making brushing motions with his hands, as if this would hasten Cameron on his way. Cameron straightened his silk doublet and locked his cold gray eyes directly with Suarez's. The scientist was the first to break away. Content in his belief that Suarez knew who was really in charge of Project Unravel, no matter what their official status, Cameron spun and walked off. He left Jessarette standing dumbly. Suarez could deal with him or not. To Cameron it made no difference now.

He had established contact in a satisfactory way. His robots had prowled this small research facility. Locked away within their incredible brains lay the full details of Suarez's DNA project. Even more important, Cameron had shown this upstart from Terra Recreations that he would not be able to operate without full consent from IM's representative.

Cameron did not know if Villalobos had intended it to be this way, but he thought so. He smiled as he walked into the bright sunlight. The gentle scent of flowers dilated his nostrils. The designers of Paradise had thought of everything. Flowers with properly pleasing scents but no insects buzzing about to annoy. Warm sunlight interspersed with gentle rains to moderate the heat gave a sense of tranquility. Everything was perfect on Paradise.

In a day or less the bioengineered virus would be loosed and alien DNA helices would begin unwrapping. Cell reproduction would cease—or even better, to Cameron's way of thinking, cell reproduction would go berserk. Blood cells would not carry oxygen. Cancers would sprout up throughout the infected's body. Metabolism would go awry. No single medicine could stop it. Viruses were notoriously difficult to isolate and destroy. The wide range of symptoms would mask the true danger since only a few cells in the alien's body would be infected.

What pleased Cameron most was the notion of killing thousands of the Bizzies. He found himself tense and shaking at the prospect. He forced himself to relax, to open his fists and flex his fingers. Killing the aliens was more than a part of the Stellar Death Plan for him. It was even more than an exercise in destruction for his prized robot hunters. Life had not been easy for him on Earth.

The damned Bizzies had made it even worse.

Cameron seethed at the ancient memories rising once more, memories he tried to keep buried. His parents, two sisters and a brother dead because an alien cargo ship refused to answer an emergency beacon when they learned it had been activated by humans. His own career stifled and almost aborted because of restrictions the aliens placed on robotic devices imported into their cultures. Most alien worlds refused to consider for purchase any product manufactured on Earth worlds. They went further. They stopped commerce in all finished goods originating on Earth, allowing only raw materials to be shipped.

The technology freeze made Cameron even angrier. The Bizzie starships were dozens, perhaps hundreds, of times faster than equivalent Earth vessels. And they refused to share the secret of their superdrive.

The alien worlds had banned together, perhaps informally, perhaps in some secret treaty, to hold back humanity.

Cameron swelled with pride knowing he helped turn the knife in a wound not yet felt by the aliens. Interstellar Materials had failed with the brain burners on Zeta Orgo, but TR's bioweapon carried with it the feel of sweet success. Cameron's only regret was that another would release it and have the satisfaction of killing untold billions of Bizarres.

As he strolled along the path, he motioned. An attentive patrolling robot surged down and hovered beside his left ear. "Where is the hunter-killer that vanished from the laboratory?" he asked. The robot had a laser trained on his lips. It was far too small to use a mechanical microphone and relied on oscillations in a different part of the EM spectrum for input.

Cameron watched from the corner of his eye as the robot emitted a coded signal only he could read. The other robot had not returned. Cameron felt no uneasiness at this. The device was one of the most intelligent robots he had fashioned. Its decision-making abilities far outstripped most humans'. He had supreme confidence that it would return when it had satisfied its urges.

His footsteps turned toward the immaculate, deserted beach stretching for kilometers along the shoreline. The brisk wind whipping off the ocean and pulling up whitecaps on the surface gave him a sense of well-being. Cameron relaxed. He had been through much and only slowly healed from the operations that had saved his life.

His hand touched the minute scars under his hairline where the surgeons had invaded his skull to relieve the pressure on his brain. Damn Kinsolving!

Even as the name crossed his mind, he reached into a pocket and pulled out the photo taken from Jessarette.

"No," Cameron said slowly as he gazed at Kinsolving's image, "you aren't dead. That fool could never kill you. Where's the proof? You are too good for him, far too clever. You will be mine one day. Oh, yes, all mine."

A worthy opponent added spring to Cameron's step, but

the sudden explosion of sea birds from behind a rock stopped him in his tracks. He looked around. His robot guards had drifted away to give him a sense of isolation—and to better survey the countryside for possible danger. Ahead he saw a tiny winking green light.

Instantly, two robot sentries moved in and hovered near him.

"What's happened?" The answer came quickly. He went to investigate personally. Dropping to the surface of a huge rock, he crawled lizardlike to the top. Pressed flat, he spied on the dozen people enjoying a small party on the other side. They danced and paired off, talking intimately, only to reform into different groupings.

Cameron almost envied them their ability to mingle so easily. But this was not his world. Any one of those cheerful people might be a killer laying a clever trap.

Even as the thought crossed his mind, he stiffened. One red-haired woman caught his attention. It took several seconds for him to recognize her as a secretary in Metchnikoff's office. Even then, he was not absolutely certain of the identification. He ordered a robot to ID her. It drifted away, then shot from sight, going straight up to form a line-of-sight computer link. It might take several minutes for the report. Cameron could wait.

"Hey, come on down and join us!" the redhead shouted, waving at him. Cameron had been seen. A moment's hesitation gripped him. If another director of Interstellar Materials had sent an aide to Paradise, that meant power struggles. Cameron could not forget the threats Metchnikoff had made at his bedside in the hospital. The director had prevented him from being appointed to IM's board.

What else did Metchnikoff have in mind? Did he hate Cameron enough to send a spy? An assassin? Cameron could not for a microsecond believe that a mere secretary, even one for a director with aspirations to be chairman, just happened to come to Paradise for a vacation at this precise instant. The expense for even a day at this planetary resort was staggering and beyond most lifetime incomes.

"Come on down. Don't be shy!" the woman called. Cameron put his robots on guard. He had to deal with this directly. He slipped over the top of the rock and landed lightly in the sand not a dozen paces from the woman.

"Thanks," he said.

"There's no need to hide when we're having such a good time. Join us," the small, frail-appearing woman invited. She cocked her head to one side, then smiled, as if suddenly remembering something pleasurable. "I know you. You work at IM, too! I've seen you around headquarters on GT."

"This is a coincidence, isn't it?" he said. "How long have you been on-planet?"

"Just arrived not two hours ago. Come on, let's dance." Cameron let her take his hand and pull him nearer to the music cube. It took him a few seconds to study the others and see how they moved. He did not enjoy dancing usually, but his superb coordination allowed him to blend in well. He found himself liking, if not actually enjoying, the sensation of his body moving smoothly once more.

"You do that well. And those are photonic clothes you've got on! Pick them up in a shop here?" she asked.

The woman's own apparel consisted mostly of a tiny gold metallic patch dangling between her legs. Cameron was not interested in her body but in whether she carried any weapons. It seemed unlikely, but his own armament required little in the way of concealment because of its smallness.

As they danced, Cameron saw tiny veins just under the skin on the woman's legs. He heaved a sigh. She had been expertly wired. The pressure of blood rushing through her blood vessels powered the transmitter. Who received the transmission? He had no idea. Metchnikoff might have sent an entire team to spy on him. Cameron wondered what the director knew about Project Unravel.

Cameron hoped that he knew nothing. Allying himself with Maria Villalobos had been dangerous. For a moment, pleasurable, but in the long run a deadly gamble on his part. The less Metchnikoff knew, the better able Cameron was to turn the project to his own ends and possibly recapture a chance at the IM directorship.

"Let's go somewhere more private," he suggested to Metchnikoff's spy.

"Private?" The woman's red hair seemed to be on fire in the intense sunlight. "All right. Where?"

"Let's just take a short walk." Cameron made a vague

gesture inland toward a small stand of trees. Hand in hand they left the others. Cameron made certain that no one took special note. Anyone in the party might be in league with the woman and Metchnikoff. That was a chance he would have to take.

"Here?" she asked, stretching out on a soft, mossy patch that seemed to have been designed for lovemaking. She propped herself up on her elbows and grinned.

Cameron walked around, eyes alert. He sent two hovering robots to patrol the area. Another monitored the output from the woman's in-body com unit. He worried at the content of the signals. She might not even know the sophisticated device had been implanted. He doubted that, but it was possible. Metchnikoff was a cunning son of a bitch. Such deception was not beyond his capacity.

"Are you going to walk in circles or are you going to . . . join me?" the woman asked. Even the tiny gold patch had twisted to one side. She seemed more naked than ever. And the wanton invitation was not one Cameron dared refuse unless he wanted to arouse her suspicions.

"What do you want from me?" he asked.

"I think that's obvious," the redhead told him, rising up and gripping his wrist. She pulled him down. Their lips met.

Cameron recoiled instantly. He had been drugged just as he had trapped Davi Jessarette! The faint taste of the woman's lip gloss lingered. He tried to rub it off.

She laughed. "That won't be good enough, Cameron. They told me the drug is efficient—and fast acting."

"But you're wearing it!"

"Special polymer between my lips and the drug. It is damned hard not to lick my lips."

Cameron's knees turned to jelly. He sank down. The woman swarmed up and on top of him. "A wonderful drug, they tell me. You can still respond. In some ways." She pulled expertly at his brightly colored clothing. "You are a handsome one. Too good for the likes of me usually. Not now."

Cameron felt himself responding to all the woman did to him. Even worse, inhibitions slipped away. The drug worked to rob him of his volition. He moaned softly as she slipped up and down his body. Another kiss insured his cooperation.

"Such a *wonderful* drug," she cooed. "Metchnikoff has never let me use it before. I promised him that this was a special case."

What the red-haired woman did to him was pleasant, but Cameron preferred having some choice. She moved faster, her fingers gripping at his sides, his shoulders. She moaned, stiffened, then relaxed, sweat dripping from her body onto his.

"That's probably the best you've ever received."

"Maria Villalobos was better," he said. "More energy. Greater expertise."

"You lying—"

"With her, I wanted it."

The woman glared at him, hatred flaring. "You can't lie, can you? No, you can't. It's impossible because of the drug. But you'd say those things just to annoy me. That's the kind of space-sucking bastard you are."

She pushed off him and towered above his supine body. "Metchnikoff wants full disclosure of Villalobos' scheme. What is happening on Paradise that requires your presence?"

Cameron thrilled at this. Metchnikoff did not know anything about Project Unravel. Some advantage might still be gained. But he felt the details rising to his lips, pulled from the most protected recesses of his mind by the insidious drug.

"Yes, my dear Cameron, tell me everything," the redhead cooed. "Then I'll have everything I need from you."

"The Plan," he gasped.

"Yes, what of it?"

His eyes blinked rapidly. The woman's face showed intense surprise. Then she toppled forward onto him. He tried to roll to one side but could not move. A tiny whir and a breath of air brought one sentry robot level with his eyes. Rapid eye blinking sent it away. Within minutes, it returned with larger, more powerful machines.

The pressure of the woman's dead body left his. Cameron watched in fascination as his robots systematically lasered the corpse into cinders, then buried the ash. He had not ordered them to do this specifically. His command had been more general: hide the body so that it cannot be found. The robots showed more initiative and inventiveness than even he, their creator, had thought possible.

A sharp pain on his thigh brought him upright. Heat sprang from the point of injection until his entire body blazed with the neutralizing drug.

Legs still shaky, he made his way through the tiny forest and returned to his distant bungalow. As he walked, strength flowed through him. With it came determination to turn this to his advantage. Metchnikoff might have several other agents on-planet. They mattered little to him now that he knew they existed.

Metchnikoff. Kinsolving. Project Unravel. It came together in a neat framework in his head. All that remained was for the touch of genius only he could bring to the situation. Before the plague ran its course, he would have a directorship in Interstellar Materials.

CHAPTER TEN

BARTON KINSOLVING fought desperately to move his arms and legs. The stench from the monster towering over him robbed him of air and took away his strength. Kinsolving held his breath, then exhaled as forcefully as he could. A small surge of power coursed through him. As the creature swiped at him with a wickedly taloned paw, he jerked to the side and rolled. He felt flesh being stripped from his back but no pain blasted into him. Kinsolving kept rolling. He heard Vandy Azmotega shouting, but her voice sounded a parsec away.

His vision narrowed until he thought he peered along a dark tunnel. Kinsolving's lungs approached the point of rupturing, but he grimly held his breath. Something about the creature's odor paralyzed. He might be robbing himself of oxygen but he also robbed the ponderous monster of a potent weapon against him.

As if the world had collapsed to a small, bright spot, Kinsolving stared up and tried to figure out what he saw. The creature bellowed and roared to one side of the small room—this was a new danger. Through his confusion and mounting agony Kinsolving recognized the flitting silver speck as the killer robot that had chased them into this room.

He could not stand but he waved his arms weakly and attracted the robot's attention. With it came the monster.

Kinsolving's strength faded too rapidly to move farther than the corner of the room. Half propped against the wall, half sprawled on the grimy floor, he watched the battle through a gathering veil of inky darkness.

Hands shook him. He tried not to breathe but his body demanded oxygen. He panted harshly and life-giving gases flowed once more into his body.

"Bart, wake up. Are you hurt?"

His eyes flickered open and focused on Vandy's face.

"We're alive?" From all he remembered, this seemed unbelievable. The monster was too big, too powerful to fight. And the stench! It had paralyzed him.

"The robot and the *friz* collided. The robot destroyed it by drilling into the creature's belly and exploding."

Kinsolving sat up and winced. His back had turned into a field of molten pain. He looked around and saw bits of dirty white and cream-colored fur, burned meat and blood spattered on walls and ceiling. The monster's carcass had been blown backward into the far wall.

"Friz?" He couldn't get his mind to work properly. He caught on the strange word and held to it, more to assure himself that he wasn't dead than to maintain a semblance of intelligence.

"The Trekans bring them along. Pets, they call them. I don't really know what they use them for. Not pets." Vandy shuddered. Bits of the creature's blood dribbled down her face. Kinsolving reached up and brushed it away; all he succeeded in doing was smearing it.

"Some pet."

"They wanted to let them run free. I stopped that when a *friz* attacked two of my staff. The Trekan who had brought it thought it was cute."

"That it hunted humans?"

Vandy only nodded. From the tight line of her lips Kinsolving knew this was still a sore point with her. Not for the first time he wondered if Cameron and the others might not be doing the right thing with their Stellar Death Plan. The aliens *did* treat humanity with contempt.

He came fully to his senses. No, the Plan was wrong. Genocide was not the answer. Earning respect in spite of the alien opposition was. Prove to them that humans were their equals. Just as were there evil humans—Kinsolving had to put Cameron and Hamilton Fremont and the others involved with the Plan in this group—so there were evil aliens. He had met those who just did their job, who were pleasant and even kind. The Zeta Orgo policeman, Quixx, was one with whom he had developed some rapport. Kinsolving wished their meeting had come under other circumstances. He felt that they might call each other friend.

Vandy helped Kinsolving to his feet. He wobbled. She

put her arm around his waist gingerly and guided him to the tunnel.

"You need an automedic. The *friz* raked your back. The wounds are shallow but the dirty claws might give you an infection."

"I couldn't move," Kinsolving said, strength returning faster now that he got out of the creature's den. "I took one breath and it reduced me to a quivering blob."

"They hunt using an airborne protein that stuns its prey. It's also part of their mating."

"Photonic," Kinsolving said sarcastically. "I don't know if it meant to eat me or mate with me."

"From all I've seen of *friz* behavior, there's not much difference. Come on, up you go." Vandy pushed him up a ladder. Kinsolving clung on and managed to emerge in the brightness of Paradise's sun. With the woman's help, he got back to her small bungalow.

"Just sit there," she said, "and I'll get the automedic over here."

"I'm doing better," Kinsolving said. He did not sit; he flopped facedown on the floor. This relieved the pressure on his wounds. He slipped off to sleep and awakened only when the buzzing robot doctor began its work.

"This will be reported," the automedic said. "Such wounds are of class three severity."

"Report them. Mark them for the same file as Steev and Gonzales."

"*Friz* wounds," the automedic agreed. With that, it spun on its axis and left.

"I won't let your name be publicly mentioned," Vandy said, "but the report to the home office has to mention you."

"Is that a smart thing to do?" asked Kinsolving. He moved his arms carefully, waiting for pain. It never came. The automedic had done its job expertly. If he hadn't experienced some stiffness, he wouldn't have known he'd been injured by the beast.

"It's part of my job. We are very careful about keeping records on such accidents. Paradise caters to a wide variety of species. Keeping one race's fun from injuring another is difficult."

"That's not what I meant. Who can you trust at Terra Recreations?"

Vandy Azmotega settled back in a padded chair and simply stared at him. She had cleaned off the *friz's* gore, changed clothes and seemed better able to concentrate on important matters. He saw the woman's face alter slightly when she realized the implications of his words.

"I resented Suarez being here, but he carried orders from my boss back on Earth. Overhearing what he plans..." Her words trailed off.

"Your boss might not know. And *his* might not. But someone at Terra Recreations authorized Suarez's work and wants him to kill all the aliens on Paradise with his bioplague. There's no way to know who sent him."

"I have nothing to do with it!" The sharp tone told of her concern and anger. Vandy had been in complete charge of the resort world until Suarez came. His Project Unravel would turn Paradise into a death planet—and this was just a minor field test. If the virus worked to expectations, it would be dumped into the atmospheres of hundreds—thousands!—of alien worlds, killing trillions of living, thinking beings.

"Never thought that you did," said Kinsolving. "But someone is responsible. Cameron was sent by a director of Interstellar Materials to observe. Knowing him, he'll end up running the project."

"Suarez is a capable man."

"He might be the best researcher in the galaxy, but Cameron is a killer. When it comes to fashioning new and more deadly robots, he is second to none."

Vandy shuddered. "We were lucky to get away from the robot in the tunnel."

"It saved me. If the *friz* hadn't attacked it, I might have been split between the two." The vision of being lasered while the *friz* ripped the flesh from his bones did not appeal to Kinsolving.

"When it doesn't return, this Cameron will be suspicious."

"Count on it," Kinsolving said. "Can you check guests to find out if anyone came with Cameron?"

Vandy reached down beside her and drew out a light wand. She aimed it at the far wall, which turned from a quaint Earth setting to a full-sized vidscreen. She worked on the light wand controls. An array of information popped onto the screen.

"See for yourself. He came alone from Gamma Tertius 4."

"Others arrived later," Kinsolving pointed out. "Two others."

Vandy worked for a few seconds, then frowned. "We can trace anyone on Paradise. Some of the pursuits requested are extremely hazardous. Mostly, the guests just want instant service."

Kinsolving said nothing. This continual spying might have reasons which satisfied most patrons, but it seemed to be unnecessary surveillance to him.

"We've lost track of Rossa Dantelli. Probes can't find her anywhere. Last tick on her was on the beach when she requested a music cube for a party."

"Who was with her then?"

"A dozen others. All human. From a variety of worlds. Her companion, Gerta Urquhart, is, uh, engaged at the moment. And was when Dantelli vanished."

"Can you track Cameron?"

"He apparently requested no service. We have honored it. But look at this." The picture dissolved and reformed. Cameron and the missing woman were together on the beach. "This was the last picture of Dantelli we recorded."

"Cameron killed her. Why?"

"Records show she is a secretary at IM headquarters."

"How does a secretary pay for such a lavish vacation?" Kinsolving wondered out loud.

"Paid for through IM accounts. Going back along the audit trails, back, back, there. Paid for from the special fund, Vladimir Metchnikoff, director."

"An internal power struggle," said Kinsolving. "That must be the reason Cameron killed her."

"We don't know he did anything to her," protested Vandy. She did not want more deaths logged as having occurred on Paradise.

"Cameron eliminates any threat. He is very efficient at his job, and his job now is Project Unravel."

Vandy said nothing, but Kinsolving knew the dilemma she faced. If she acted against Cameron and Suarez, she took the chance of losing not only her job but her life. Someone superior to her had authorized Project Unravel. Who? She had no way of knowing.

"This," she said, "might not go all the way to TR's board. Some junior officers might have given Suarez the funds. Who knows how much is in slush funds that are never directly accounted for."

"It infects IM's board," Kinsolving said, trying to show her the full extent of the Plan. "Fremont is the leading proponent of alien genocide there. The Plan is a secret to most employees, but not to IM's board. I'm wondering if the same is true for Terra Recreations."

"No," Vandy said. "I can't believe that. Our chairman has always sought out alien contacts. He opened Paradise to other species over a split vote. They had to go to a shareholders' meeting for final approval."

"We might identify some of the conspirators in the Stellar Death Plan by looking at that vote," said Kinsolving.

Vandy turned paler. "The director of my section voted against an open-species policy, but that doesn't mean he is part of any plot to murder entire planets!"

"No," agreed Kinsolving. "It doesn't. It just makes it more difficult knowing who to trust. Anyone might—or might not—be involved. Can you contact the chairman directly?"

"I can try. I'll send a special courier right away." Vandy paused, shaking her head. "What do I say? That another Earth company has assassins on Paradise killing each other and they're waiting for one of our scientists to slaughter almost fourteen hundred aliens with a bioengineered virus? He'd suspend me for indulging in some of our more mind-bending diversions."

"Send a courier you can trust with the message," said Kinsolving. That would not be enough. It might take weeks for the warning to be delivered and even more weeks for a positive response. Even worse, there might be no response at all—or Vandy might discover everyone at TR was implicated in the Plan. Whatever had to be done to save the aliens on Paradise had to be done soon.

Barton Kinsolving would have to do it. But what?

CHAPTER ELEVEN

CAMERON STARED at the spot in the small forest where Metchnikoff's assassin had been buried by the robots. He worried over the information lost by the woman's abrupt death, but he remembered the faint drug tingle on his lips. He had been given no opportunity to question her. Cameron hadn't even learned her name, as if that were important. Killing those who tried to kill him carried with it some small pleasure. He had triumphed, she had died. Simple.

But he needed information. Suarez would prove reluctant, Cameron knew, to obey. Suarez thought he worked for others in the TR hierarchy. That had ended when Villalobos sent Cameron to Paradise. Cameron would take charge of this ingenious weapon, whether anyone working for Terra Recreations wanted it that way or not.

"What others might Metchnikoff have sent?" he asked aloud. A thick aerial robot whizzed up and came to a halt in front of him. On a small one-line screen mounted in its side, the robot disgorged information almost faster than Cameron could read it.

"Gerta Urquhart," he mused. "Metchnikoff's other spy. Should I remove her immediately? No, I should save her. Let her wonder what happened to her friend." Cameron smiled broadly. He liked the idea of making Metchnikoff's spies suffer. Rubbing his lips, Cameron started away from the unmarked grave and walked toward the beach. Halfway to the water he stopped, turned and blew a soft kiss to his fallen opponent. She had not been very good, either as a spy or as a lover, but she had worked for IM. She deserved that much.

Cameron motioned and the information-carrying robot moved to a position where he could more easily read the rest of the report. The infobot had accomplished its task—partially. The part he needed most was missing.

"Nothing on Kinsolving's whereabouts, eh? But we have enough to find Lark Versalles. Where?" He studied the single line as it flashed the answer. Cameron continued walking along the beach, enjoying the soft sea breeze and the sharp tang of salt in the air, then abruptly turned and went inland.

He felt the pressure of time mounting. He had so much to do and so little time. The narrow pathway he found led him to a grassy meadow dotted with billowing particolored silk tents. It might have been a scene out of some medieval adventure except for the omnipresent metallic servants hovering nearby to cater to the guests' every whim.

Cameron allowed his own robotic guardians to drift further away in their patrols. He halted and studied the people gathered in the middle of the meadow. He had no trouble picking out Lark Versalles in the crowd. Her cosmetic dyes reflected ever-shifting patterns of silvers and gold in the noonday sun. Cameron skirted the group, approaching Lark from behind. She had her arm around another woman as they watched a group of gaily painted dancers performing acrobatic feats that defied both gravity and anatomy.

He had hoped to find Kinsolving with Lark. That the cause of Cameron's problems was not present did not bother him unduly. The hunt was always the sweeter when the prey proved exceptionally astute.

". . . so good!" squealed Lark. She turned and kissed her companion full on the lips.

Cameron frowned. Lark's companion appeared to be a human female but subtle indications to the contrary worked at the corners of his mind.

"Report," he said. The infobot flashed a single name: Onar.

Cameron went cold inside. Lark had taken a Bizzie lover. Lark Versalles was stunningly beautiful, but with that beauty went a decadence that sickened Cameron. How could she make love to a creature as much male as it was female? This miscegenation only fueled Cameron's hatred. People like Lark Versalles had to be saved from their own base instincts. Dealing with the aliens because of business pressure was one thing. Having social—sexual—relations transcended necessity.

He would be interested in seeing how effective Dr.

Suarez's virus was against Onarians. If it proved ineffectual, Cameron vowed to remove the Bizzie himself. Lark was too fine a woman to waste on aliens.

What would her family say?

Cameron pulled his attention from the pair and scanned the crowd. He did not find Kinsolving, either in disguise or hiding in some other fashion. But then he had not expected to. His robot had already scanned the crowd and identified them. Most were from Earth, children of rich parents out for a few brief and diverting days of vacation. Others bought their way to Paradise with more illicit funds. Cameron recognized two assassins working for other companies and a freelance killer whose reputation exceeded her ability. Of Gerta Urquhart he saw no sign.

A tiny flash from a robot alerted him. He said softly into a pickup mike under his lapel, "I will be there within five minutes." Cameron turned and walked away from the dance troupe. For such frivolous art he had no time. His art matched his craft; well-designed circuits, innovative AI contrivances, robots undreamed of by others. And smaller. Always smaller by half.

The brisk walk upslope took him to another path. He maintained his steady progress until he came to the small building housing Suarez's underground laboratory. Davi Jessarette stood guard outside, arms crossed and a sullen expression clouding his ugly face.

Cameron had expected him. Two patrolling survey robots had already reported the assassin's presence before he had come into view.

"Suarez is waiting for you," Jessarette said. The sour expression and his tone showed that he felt betrayed. He had trusted Cameron and been turned into a robot to be ordered around. Cameron wondered if Suarez had neutralized the night juggler drug or if he had allowed it to wear off. If the latter, Jessarette would have experienced severe spasms and stomach cramps.

"I'm aware of that. He signalled me directly."

Cameron moved quickly as Jessarette opened the door. A slight shift in weight and Cameron slipped past Jessarette, making it seem as if the other killer had been reduced to opening doors. Cameron donned his vid goggles and touched one temple. A view of all that happened behind him flashed across the special lenses without impairing his forward vision. He saw Jessarette reach for his weapon, then reconsider.

Cameron's back presented a good target. Too good. Jessarette looked around and saw no fewer than ten robots trailing behind their master. The man relaxed and moved his hand away from his weapon.

Cameron tried not to laugh out loud. None of the ten robots would have fired. Not when one had attached itself to Jessarette's collar. The slightest muscular tension signalling real danger would be acted upon by that robot. The small explosive charge would blow off Jessarette's head before the signal to squeeze a trigger could be sent from brain to finger.

Cameron considered ordering his killer robot to detonate and put Jessarette out of his misery. The man suffered and did not know the reason. Cameron decided to allow the pathetic man to live for a little longer. Jessarette's death should serve a purpose other than simple whim gratification.

"Doctor," Cameron called out, "when will you release the virus?"

"I wanted to give a brief report, Cameron," Morgan Suarez said, "because it seems to be expected in higher circles. You are not in charge of this project."

"Report," Cameron said crisply. He saw Jessarette stiffen but the muscles along the man's shoulders did not tighten in the way indicating that he would draw his weapon.

Suarez's dark eyes burned with anger. "I have completed the preliminary production. We have enough virus to infect the fourteen hundred plus Bizzies currently on Paradise."

"Then release the virus. Why delay?"

"The delivery mechanism must be precise. We need complete and accurate information at every stage of the infection. I will release it slowly, in specific populations of aliens. We are not equipped to study more than two or three at a time."

"You have fourteen hundred Bizzies from a dozen or more species as your test subject and you're only going to use it on two or three?" Cameron shook his head in disapproval.

"This is not an actual attack, Cameron. It is a field test—nothing more."

"Then, by all means, let us *test*."

Suarez's assistant shouted and dived for the table containing the vials of bioengineered death. A second shout terminated suddenly as a laser beam drilled through the side of the man's head. He fell facedown on the floor, fingers fastened on the edge of the table.

"This is an outrage!" cried Suarez.

"He tried to prevent my robot from ... appropriating your virus."

"What are you doing? Stop it!"

"Really, doctor, I am only doing what you said you'd do if you had the equipment. My robot has an aerosol spray attachment. It is loaded with eighty milliliters of distilled water now infected with your virus. The remaining twenty milliliters from the vial is untouched."

"You don't know what you're doing. We need to study." Morgan Suarez took a step toward Cameron. An angry buzzing from a guard robot froze the scientist. "You dare to threaten me!"

"I, sir? Not at all. I am merely doing as Director Villalobos instructed. I am here to make sure that the proper tests are conducted. You worry needlessly. We are not adversaries. Rather, we are on the same side."

Cameron wondered if that were true of Davi Jessarette but did not include him in company of those adhering to the Stellar Death Plan.

"Where is it going?" demanded Suarez when he saw the thick cylinder of the robot floating out of the room. To Jessarette he shouted, "Stop it! This fool will ruin the test!"

"Davi," Cameron said in a soft voice. "You will die if you try to obey him. He seems to have forgotten why we are all here."

"But the vice president in charge of Paradise told me to do whatever Dr. Suarez said," the man protested.

Cameron filed away the information. He had no inkling of those involved with the Plan in other companies. Even within the IM ranks, he knew of only a few.

"You will be carrying out the vice president's wishes

more fully by doing nothing." In a voice even softer and infinitely more deadly, he added, "That is because you will still be alive."

"Jessarette," hissed Suarez.

"Enough." Cameron moved to the monitoring panel Suarez had set up for the test. Two small vidscreens showed inside a Bizzie compound. The lizardlike aliens lounged at the edge of a boiling hot pool of mud. He studied the scene and decided that Suarez had smuggled in two rice-grain cameras for the surveillance. He did not quite sneer at such primitive equipment but his opinion of the researcher dropped several degrees. Morgan Suarez might be a genius with recombinant bioweapons but his electronic expertise was positively twentieth century.

"I have positioned more than twenty aerial cameras at altitudes ranging from one kilometer up to fifty kilometers above the planet," he told Suarez. "These will provide continuous viewing and give the most minute details possible of the infectious process."

"Impossible. I need sharp definition. I need..." Suarez's voice trailed off when he saw the vidscreen. The picture showed a lounging reptile so distinct that he might have been looking through a visual microscope.

"Closer?" Cameron gestured. The texture of the rough alien skin turned into mountains and valleys more appropriate on the surface of a planet. "More?" The very pores in the skin opened. "This is taken with an electronic camera two kilometers overhead. I can bring in a close-up. It's not quite as good as a scanning electron microscope at that range, but it is good."

"This is incredible. I never knew it was possible."

"This is adequate? I can monitor forty channels simultaneously. It is all being fed into your computer for analysis."

Suarez looked at Cameron. "And is being recorded for your own use?"

"Mine? I have no use for this. The Plan must be served, and Interstellar Materials is intimately involved with the Plan."

"How are you proposing to release the virus? It must be done slowly, and in precise amounts."

"Down to a microliter? My robot sprayer can oblige."

"Do it. On this compound, four microliters at an altitude of ten meters."

"Done," said Cameron. He pointed to the controls for the spraying robot and let Suarez work on his own.

Within an hour the entire load of deadly virus had been precisely delivered to the most opportune targets. All that remained was data collection—and alien death.

CHAPTER TWELVE

"NO," VANDY AZMOTEGA SAID, shaking her head vigorously. "It matches everything I've seen and heard, but it is too fantastic."

"You were the one who said that alien guests were dying. Is that the reputation you want for your resort?" Kinsolving knew the battle Vandy was fighting inside. She had to be convinced that Terra Recreations had authorized murder to test a bioweapon. He guessed that her association with TR had been nothing but pleasant until this moment.

"Cameron. Maybe he has corrupted Suarez."

"You heard them. Who came to Paradise to observe? Suarez had his project well under way before Cameron arrived." Kinsolving lounged back, wincing slightly. The numbing anesthetic had begun to wear off; his back burned as though someone had run a laser over it burning in parallel grooves.

"Why should I trust you?"

Kinsolving heaved a deep breath. "You probably shouldn't. This might prejudice you against me, but you deserve the full truth. I was supervisor on Deepdig, a planet IM leased from the Lorr. I discovered massive losses in the rare earth ores. Tracing them, my . . . I found that my assistant was responsible."

"Your assistant?" probed Vandy. Her eyes burned.

"My lover, too. Ala Markken. At least I have reason to believe she was responsible for the thefts and that she tried to kill me. And that she knows about the Plan."

Vandy studied him critically. Kinsolving shoved to his feet and walked to the window. For a moment he swayed, off balance. The small house seemed out of place in a world of opulence, but Vandy allowed herself some luxuries. The view was not of Paradise but an Earth ocean smashing against a rocky cliff. He had not expected the appearance of a sheer drop just centimeters away.

"The rare earths were siphoned off and used in the brain burners. A single crystal of cerium oscillating at the appropriate frequency acts like a drug for some alien species." Kinsolving turned from the window and faced Vandy. "There is more."

"It has something to do with Lark Versalles?"

"No," he said impatiently. "More. Cameron made it appear that I had murdered a Lorr official. He did it, but I was sentenced to exile. Lark happened along and rescued me. A chance in a million. The Lorr are looking for me as an escaped murderer. Cameron wants me for the sheer joy of killing me. Anyone having to do with the Stellar Death Plan would cheerfully kill me, too."

"That's all I needed to know."

"What?"

"I intercepted a message packet routed through IM channels. You carry a hefty reward on your head. And a few months ago the Lorr left a photo facsimile of you. I routinely circulated it among the security staff. The Lorr are hunting you, Bart. Actively. You seem to have stung their pride."

"A mere human escaping a prison world where no one has ever escaped? I should think that would do it."

"You could kill," Vandy said.

"I have. But I didn't kill the Lorr."

Kinsolving saw that the woman had decided. She had accumulated enough facts, sifted through them, mixed in her own feelings and come to a conclusion. Running a resort planet like Paradise did not permit the luxury of protracted decision making.

"We've got to find Cameron and stop him," she said. "My security force is not up to the task. Not since any of them might be working with Suarez." She swallowed hard. "It's obvious to me that Jessarette saw your photo and tried to kill you on Almost Paradise. He might have heard something about you and Cameron. He's always shown good intelligence-gathering skills."

"Cameron would be far harder to capture—or kill— than Suarez," said Kinsolving, going to the heart of the real problem facing them. "We should find the virus and destroy it. But there will be some problems."

"Death, for one," said Vandy. "You don't have to convince me how dangerous this is. But there's one factor in our favor: I'm still in charge of Paradise, and I command all its resources. An entire planet is a powerful force."

Kinsolving did not want to discourage her. They both needed confidence that they might succeed, but he had the gut level feeling that Cameron's cleverness had already undercut much of Vandy's power.

"Try the computer banks," he requested. "Track Suarez and see if you can even locate Cameron."

She lifted the light wand and pointed it at a few key toggles on the wall vidscreen. A flash and then . . . nothing.

Vandy frowned. "Hard to believe it's out of order. I just had the entire system maintenanced a month ago."

"See if you can locate Jessarette. I can't believe Cameron held him in too high a regard. He seemed to be drugged in the lab."

"Davi Jessarette's not too bright but he has his uses. Some guests become rowdy and require a human touch. Not everything can be done using robots."

"There," Kinsolving cried when an aerial scan of a crowd panned past Jessarette. "And that's Suarez with him."

"I still can't lock on Suarez. It's as if the computer refuses to acknowledge his existence, yet we can see him."

"Do another check. Cameron has been tinkering with your computer banks." Kinsolving moved closer to the vidscreen and peered at the two men. The researcher used a small, hand-held device to sample the air.

"Bart, he might be releasing the virus!"

Kinsolving experienced a moment's nausea. "No," he said. "They've already released it. He's sampling the air to see how effective the virus is."

"Let's go find out for ourselves," Vandy said. She reached into a cabinet and pulled out an impact laser. "Can you use this thing? I've had it for years and never even fired it."

"I learn quick," Kinsolving said. He checked the charge levels. The small laser locked onto target, then fired, rapidly varying the lasing frequency. No energy weapon had stopping power, but the impact laser came close as it produced a differential heating zone in its target. With luck, it would duplicate the impact of a small explosive projectile. At worst, it burned the hell out of its target.

"Down on the sward. We were duplicating a medieval fair. The aliens tend to like it more than our Earth guests. Shows how primitive we really are."

Kinsolving and Vandy hurried along the deserted paths, taking one that only service personnel used. "There," Vandy said. "A cab. One of ten we keep nearby for getting around when we need to. Otherwise, we walk or let the robots carry our supplies."

Kinsolving jumped into the small cab and pulled the plastic air shield down. Vandy slipped into the seat beside him and pressed her key card into the ignition. For a moment, Kinsolving tried to figure out what was bothering him. Dozens of observations came crashing together in his mind and formed a deadly picture. He yanked out the impact laser and used it on the air shield. It exploded in a molten burst. Vandy protested but he cut her short, grabbing her arm and pulling her through the fiery-rimmed hole he had just burned.

The cab erupted in a sheet of searing orange flame seconds after they had exited. A powerful hand plucked at his body, lifting, tearing, turning. Kinsolving landed heavily, moaning because he had opened the wounds on his back by sliding along the ground.

"What happened? I never saw anything like that before."

Kinsolving levered himself to a sitting position. "Cameron is efficient. When I locked the air shield down, I noticed two newly installed block circuit connections. The one circuit hummed when you used your key card. Anyone else could use the cab with no trouble. Your identicard triggered the bomb."

"Cameron knows?"

"He must. His robots are everywhere."

"Why wouldn't he simply kill me? If the robot killers are as good as you say, why not just use them?"

"How can you explain a cat playing with a mouse? He thinks he is in control." Kinsolving sat and thought hard. "It might be something else, though. I've kept a low profile since Jessarette tried to kill me on Almost Paradise. This might be his doing. Cameron wants me, and Jessarette thinks using you as bait is the way to finish what he started and show Cameron up at the same time."

"He came damned close," Vandy said. She brushed smoldering plastic from her hair, then checked to be sure she hadn't missed any. "If we split forces, though, we weaken our position. I have access to anywhere on-planet. And you know more about Cameron than I could learn in a few minutes."

"Let's walk. If we can get to Suarez, we might find out something about stopping the virus."

Kinsolving doubted it but they had to do something. If Suarez had released the recombinant DNA airborne weapon there might be nothing that anyone could do until it had run its course—killing untold numbers of aliens on Paradise.

Panting, sweat running in salty rivers down his back and burning his wounds, Kinsolving found himself hard-pressed to keep up with Vandy as they ran through the sylvan glades and thick, well-tended forests. He about doubled over from exhaustion when they emerged from a copse and looked down the grassy slope to where Suarez and Jessarette still stood.

"What now?" asked Vandy. "Shoot them with the laser?"

"They deserve it, but we need information, not retribution. Even if they've released it, there might be an antidote or something that will kill the virus before it can work."

"Bart, Jessarette has spotted us!"

He saw that Vandy was right. Davi Jessarette tugged at Suarez's arm and pointed upslope in their direction.

"We can't reach them before they melt into the crowd," said Vandy, her sharp eyes judging distances and speeds.

"Let's see if I can herd them away," said Kinsolving. He pulled out the impact laser and sent the faint red sighting beam out to a spot halfway between the men and the bulk of the crowd gathered for the medieval exhibition. He triggered the laser. A rock exploded at Jessarette's feet, sending the man stumbling back.

"You missed!" cried Vandy.

"All I want to do is keep them away from the others."

Kinsolving fired again. Jessarette had drawn a weapon of his own. Suarez yelled something that turned into a muffled shout of anger by the time it reached Kinsolving, but the intent was crystalline. He wanted Jessarette to remove the danger.

Kinsolving tried to hit Jessarette's legs and missed. Jessarette moved quickly and well to avoid becoming a good target. Kinsolving's experience with combat weapons was limited. Jessarette did far better with his own weapon.

A sudden glint as Jessarette fired it gave Kinsolving all the warning he was likely to receive.

"Vandy, into the forest. Hurry. *Now!*" He had thought to drive Suarez and Jessarette away from sanctuary in the crowd gathered for the medieval spectacle. A single shot had turned his strategy against them. They were now the pursued instead of the pursuers.

"What's wrong?" she demanded. "What happened?"

Kinsolving glanced over his shoulder and caught a second glimpse of sunlight reflected off a long, slender projectile.

"One of Cameron's toys," he panted. Already he was short of breath. He had come too far too fast to be in good shape. Kinsolving jerked Vandy to the left, ducked, turned and tried to run at an angle. A snapping sound came from behind. An overhanging branch limb burst into flame. The pursuing robot's laser had ignited the dried wood.

Kinsolving sensed rather than saw the danger. He shoved Vandy sprawling as he whipped around, his own laser up and struggling to find a target. The tiny robot proved too elusive a target. He fired and missed. The robot fired—and struck.

Kinsolving yelled in pain. His hand trembled too much for him to properly aim with the impact laser's sighting beam. The pursuing robot whirred around in an orbit so fast that Kinsolving knew he was doomed.

"Bart!" Vandy Azmotega stood and took a step toward him.

"Keep down!" he shouted, but it was too late. The robot spun on its axis and aimed its deadly laser directly for Vandy's head.

CHAPTER THIRTEEN

KINSOLVING WAS NOT even aware of acting. He pointed the impact laser in the general direction of the robot and fired repeatedly. One shot might have struck it; the ionization cloud from the laser discharge might have disrupted vital circuits; the robot might have damaged itself in its flight through the forest. Whatever the cause, the robot exploded, showering Vandy and Kinsolving with a molten rain of sundered parts.

He lay back on the ground, stunned. Shaking off the effects, he rolled and came to his feet. Vandy Azmotega struggled to stand. She, too, had been dazed by the blast.

"You're either a damned good shot or luckier than you have any right to be," she said. "Help me up."

He gave her a hand and said, "I don't know much about assassin projectiles. This might be a standard issue, but I don't think so. If it is one of Cameron's, he already knows it failed."

"You think he'll send another?"

"He might send a thousand." Kinsolving looked up through the green leaves to the azure sky. He had no way of knowing what Cameron would do. The man had been on Paradise long enough to have a million self-contained, deadly, thinking robots everywhere.

"We can't let this stop us," Vandy said. "Paradise's reputation is at stake. Suarez can't be allowed to kill guests." She sounded more aggrieved about the pleasure planet's reputation than the lives of her guests, but Kinsolving understood her sentiments.

"Jessarette and Suarez will be long gone," he said. "Where is the nearest enclave of aliens? You said Jessarette had been guarding the ambassador. They might have used Jessarette to get past the Trekans' own security system."

"This way." Vandy wobbled a little, then walked with her usual firm, brisk stride through the forest. Kinsolving held back, letting her go first. His dark eyes scanned the branches and open spaces for the slightest hint of another laser-equipped robot.

He saw nothing, and this worried him more than finding an entire flock of metallic killers. Was Cameron toying with him or was this part of some grander, more devious scheme? Cameron could not have known he would come across Kinsolving on Paradise. Kinsolving had not known where he shifted when he fled Zeta Orgo 4.

Coincidence? Or destiny? Kinsolving tried not to believe in destiny or luck, yet his continued existence worked to erode his disbelief. Escaping the Lorr prison had been luck. The only parts that had been skill lay in keeping alive. Even discovering the details of the Plan had been accidental.

If accident had put him on this strange and dangerous path, only clever planning and ability would keep him alive.

"They had sensors placed around their compound to keep out casual interlopers," Vandy said. "I know where they are and how they work. I insisted on knowing. This way."

She traced a complicated path across an innocuous-appearing lawn until Kinsolving called to her to stop. "Show me one of the sensors."

Vandy silently pointed to a small mound in the grass. Kinsolving knelt and brushed the mosslike grass back, exposing the dirt. Careful prying lifted the device.

"Their guards will be all over us," she said tiredly. "We should have announced our arrival. Maybe I can tell the ambassador that you're a tech doing some repair work."

"No need. A new circuit has been built into the sensor, circumventing its function."

"Cameron?"

"I don't think so. This is sloppy work. I saw it instantly; anyone would. Someone else has been plying their trade, and not doing it nearly as well as Cameron."

"You found Cameron's booby trap in the cab."

"That was substandard work, too. Better than this, but not up to his exacting detail. Is Jessarette capable of such work?" He held up the sensor for her inspection. Vandy shrugged.

"He might be. I never got good work from him, but he never really failed, either. His profile shows that he has a higher opinion of his abilities than reality warrants." She gave a strange little laugh. "That's nothing. Most of us on Paradise have the same notation on our psych profiles. Goes with the work of satisfying other people's fantasies."

Kinsolving dropped the gimmicked sensor. Jessarette had a hand in much of what had happened. He had guarded Morgan Suarez and had been in charge of the Trekan ambassador. Kinsolving felt a tightening in his belly. Jessarette might be the stumbling block more than Cameron. If so, they had a chance. Cameron made few mistakes—and those had already been committed. The foppish assassin never made the same mistake twice.

"No guards along the walls?" Kinsolving strained to see the top of the shoulder-high rock wall. "Not even any vidcameras?"

"Full array. Hidden to keep the guests from feeling imprisoned," answered Vandy, but the tone she used showed worry. She walked along the wall and opened a hidden junction box.

"Let me guess," said Kinsolving. "All the circuits are gimmicked."

"A relay transmitter, too. Whatever is seen is broadcast to an unauthorized location. We use fiber optic cables to prevent eavesdropping. This is all added."

Kinsolving wiggled to the top of the wall and then dropped over, expecting fiery beams to cross in the center of his chest. Nothing. Vandy followed him over rather than going the hundred meters along the wall to the front gate.

"Fancy building," Kinsolving said. He had worked in the mines most of his life and was unused to luxury in any form. Even these alien palaces struck him as extraordinary.

"We try to please," Vandy said. She grabbed his arm and stopped him, head canted to one side and a look of extreme concern on her face.

For a few seconds Kinsolving wondered what troubled her. Then he heard it, too. At first, it was faint, almost too vague to hear. Then it came in a roar that equalled any physical blow he had ever received. If an entire zoo had been turned loose, the cacophony of barks and whistles and howls of rage and pain could not have matched it.

"The ambassador," Vandy said in a weak voice.

Kinsolving would not have recognized the creature that burst from the mansion doors as sentient if she had not warned him. Fiery red eyes blazed as the beast rushed across the lawn toward them. Fingers hooked like talons raked the air. Worst of all was the demented shrieking.

"The laser, Bart. Use the laser!" Vandy cried, when it became obvious that they were the rampaging Trekan's target.

Kinsolving reacted too slowly. Shock at seeing such a wild being prevented him from responding with the deadly bolt that would have snuffed out a life. By the time he recovered, it was too late to use the laser. The ambassador from a civilized and sophisticated world ripped and tore at him like a rabid dog.

Kinsolving and the alien tumbled to the ground and rolled, the laser falling from Kinsolving's grip. Kinsolving came out on top and used his superior weight to hold the ambassador's shoulders down. His face pressed close to the Trekan's. Kinsolving wished he dared release the alien. The Trekan's face looked more like a pale green dog's than a human's. The long snout protruded only half as long as an Earth canine's, but the teeth were definitely a carnivore's. Above the lips, pulled back in a feral snarl, were tiny pockets of what appeared to be pus. One sac burst and yellow ichor dribbled down the ambassador's cheek. Wherever the liquid touched it burned.

"Easy, keep calm," Kinsolving urged. The Trekan was beyond reason. Froth speckled his lips. He surged again and sent Kinsolving flying. Seldom had Kinsolving felt such berserk power—and never directed against him by such a small being.

The Trekan dropped to all fours as if denying ten million years of evolution. Eyes turned to slits, the alien shuffled forward. Kinsolving had no strength left. He had fought too many battles.

The ambassador gasped, let out an all too human sigh, then sagged to one side.

"What happened?" asked Vandy. She had picked up Kinsolving's fallen impact laser. "I started to fire, but he keeled over before I did."

"He's dead." Kinsolving carefully avoided contact with the ichorous sores.

"The virus?" Vandy's words were muffled by a gentle breeze blowing from the direction of the mansion.

"I'm afraid so." Kinsolving sniffed and detected an odor that gagged him. It took incredible determination but he walked slowly to the mansion door through which the ambassador had come and peered inside.

His reflexes saved him. He had the impact laser up and firing before he realized what he was doing. Two Trekans exploded as if miniature suns had blossomed in their chests. Kinsolving recoiled and ran into Vandy, who stood and stared, openmouthed.

"I've never seen anything like this. I thought I had seen it all, but this!" She shook her head, sending a soft auburn cascade down around her shoulders. Kinsolving fixed his gaze on her hair—human hair, normal, natural, something to stroke and enjoy and normal, normal, not like the hideous scene within.

"They're all dead. The virus is doing this to them. Turning them insane. It must affect the neurochemicals in their brains."

"The limbic system. It's taken over conscious thought. Their physiology is similiar to ours," said Vandy. "I have complete workups on them. On all the aliens." She swallowed hard. The paleness of her face made Kinsolving wonder if she was about to faint.

The dizziness he felt made him wonder if *he* was about to faint.

"The neurotransmitters are failing," she said. "The chemicals that allow the Trekans to think like civilized people aren't being reproduced. That must be it."

"But the sores. Those can't be natural."

Vandy shook her head. "Who knows what Suarez has loosed on my planet. Damn him! I'll stuff him down a black hole when I find him!"

"Is there another compound nearby? Other aliens?" Kinsolving was afraid of what they might find, but he had to look. There might be a small chance of saving some of the fourteen hundred aliens on Paradise.

He did not really think it was possible, though, not after seeing what the Trekans had become.

A PLAGUE IN PARADISE   107

Vandy Azmotega led the way across the field and to another dazzling white marble palace set high atop a hill. From the side Kinsolving saw the ocean's waves crashing into the sandy shoreline. This was an idyllic place to sit and relax, but he got no sense of serenity. The mansion was preternaturally quiet. The Treka household had been noisy as the beasts within each civilized creature had been set free to roam. He heard no sound here other than the wind and water.

"How awful," gasped Vandy.

Kinsolving had steeled himself for what they might find. This exceeded his worst expectations. He could not even identify the species of alien. Each had died in horrible pain.

"They broke every bone in their bodies trying to—what?" asked Vandy.

"Hallucinations? Pain? Who knows what Project Unravel did to them," Kinsolving said bitterly. "This is the legacy the Stellar Death Plan will give the universe."

"How can they?" moaned Vandy. "If they see how hideous this is, they'll stop. They have to!"

"They won't," Kinsolving said. "I doubt this affects Suarez at all. Maybe he's happy at the efficient way of killing he's found. He might be displeased if it didn't work fast enough or on every alien."

Vandy turned and ran from the mansion. Kinsolving held his gorge down as he followed behind her. Putrescence would soon set in, turning these fabulous houses into charnel pits.

He could not allow anyone advocating annihilation of all aliens to continue along this path. He had to stop those behind the Plan.

Barton Kinsolving stopped a few paces from where Vandy Azmotega hunched over, trying vainly to regain her composure. He looked up and saw a flash of light against the bright blue sky. Kinsolving lifted the impact laser and carefully aimed. He had to take a dozen shots before he hit the weaving, dodging robot.

It crashed to the ground a few meters distant.

"That's it," he told Vandy. "They used robots—probably that very one—to spray the virus into the air where the aliens inhaled it." He directed the aiming beam to the center of the partially destroyed machine. A final laser blast completely destroyed the aerosol spraying robot.

The booby traps might have been Jessarette's work. Kinsolving recognized a master's design in this machine.

Cameron had just delivered the virus that destroyed fourteen hundred living, breathing, thinking beings.

CHAPTER FOURTEEN

KINSOLVING STARED at the vidscreen, not seeing the three-dimensional parade of faces and figures. Vandy Azmotega muttered constantly to herself and she worked to bring her computer banks under full control again. The harder she worked, the more she failed.

"I give up. I thought I knew the system, but there's no way I can get the scanners to pick up Suarez. As for Cameron, the vidcams won't even register his bungalow, much less him. Imagine that!"

"He's good," Kinsolving said, still distracted. Too much had happened. The virus had worked rapidly and with a vicious effectiveness. He hoped that Vandy would not do another quick-scan of the alien quarters. The crews she had dispatched worked with remotes to prevent further contamination, but Kinsolving knew that no human could catch the plague that had destroyed so many others.

It had been specifically designed to kill only Bizarres.

"I even did a complete program wipe and reinstalled. Nothing works as it should," complained Vandy. "It's almost as if he had access to system level."

"Considering how expert Cameron is, he might have designed the system you use." Kinsolving sat upright, ignoring the momentary pain in his back. He made a mental note to have the automedic take another look at his injuries. They should have completely healed by now. But a disturbing thought intruded.

"Can you punch up every other guest on Paradise?" he asked. "Locate Lark Versalles for me."

"Lark?" Vandy's tone indicated what she thought of the other woman. She pointed her light wand at the vidscreen and a kaleidoscopic twisting brought Lark's face into sharp focus. The cosmetic dyes appeared muted and even somber in their olive drabs and beiges. Kinsolving hardly recognized her because of that.

"Can you contact her and have her come here?"

Vandy tapped in a new command to the light wand. Lark's image jumped. Vandy had not brought up the sound but Kinsolving saw from Lark's frightened expression that a voice spoke from thin air. This could not be the source of Lark's discomfort.

"Pan," he ordered. "Stop! There. Look at her. Sheeda. I had forgotten about her. She's an alien. An Onarian."

"She's not dead, though," Vandy said, more curious than irritated now. She used the light wand to issue new commands. On-screen Kinsolving saw a contamination-suited staff worker enter and place Sheeda on a mobile stretcher. Lark followed behind the floating stretcher, wringing her hands and looking increasingly miserable.

Within ten minutes the door chimes sounded. Kinsolving let the trio in. "Put her over there," he told the suited man, indicating a spot for Sheeda's stretcher.

"Bart, darling!" cried Lark when she saw him. She threw her arms around his neck and buried her face in his shoulder. Hot tears burned through his shirt. "Something happened to Sheeda. No one will get her a doctor. She's dying, Bart!"

"I'm afraid so," he said gently. He stroked her fine hair. She had changed its color since he had seen her last. Stripes of verdant green and fuchsia turned her into something both clownish and exotic. "This is Cameron's doing."

"Barton, no! He wouldn't..." Lark's voice trailed off. She knew differently. "That son of a bitch. I'll shove him feet-first into a plasma torch!"

"This isn't the first time he's killed your friends," he said. "Remember back on Gamma Tertius 4? Dinky and the others? And how his robots killed Randi duLong aboard ship? This time he's released a plague killing only aliens."

"But Sheeda hasn't done anything to him. Why does he want to hurt her?"

"Prejudice isn't rational," he said, knowing this was not what Lark wanted to hear. But Kinsolving had no words to comfort her. For all the uneasiness he felt in Sheeda's presence, he wished the dual-sexed Onarian no harm.

Vandy had started her automedic working on Sheeda. The alien lay on the stretcher, as pale as death and in a light coma. Occasionally her eyes opened but no intelligence shone forth. The glaze made Kinsolving think that the woman/man endured a fever of incredible proportions, even though the automedic recorded normal temperature levels.

"The robot's doing a full workup now," said Vandy. "Sheeda might be the only alien left on Paradise. I've scanned all the guests and haven't found any others alive."

"No one knew about this," said Lark, still in shock. "The others. The humans. They... they didn't say a word."

"As far as our Earth guests are concerned, nothing *has* happened," answered Vandy. "We'd like to keep it that way. But I've had to shift out message packets to the aliens' home worlds. It will be a few weeks before answers come back—probably as indignant delegations wanting to sever diplomatic ties with Earth for such an atrocity."

"A few weeks," mused Kinsolving. "By then IM will know of the success. Cameron will have sent back a message packet to GT4."

"I've interdicted all messages except for those I approve," said Vandy, as if she thought Kinsolving were a fool for not believing her capable of doing her job. Then his meaning struck her as hard as a blow to the jaw. "Cameron can send whatever he wants. He has control of my computer."

"And anything else he wants on Paradise. But he might not trust his report to a packet. This news is something he might want to deliver in person."

"The automedic's finished," cut in Lark. "What does it say? Is Sheeda all right?"

Kinsolving scanned the report. He had been trained to work with field automedic units on Deepdig. Interpreting the robotic results had been part of that training. He shook his head. "This only shows a chemical imbalance in her system. The automedic isn't equipped for full alien biochemistry workups. But I think we can keep her alive. Not repair the damage done, perhaps, but keep her alive until we can ship her back to Onar for proper medical help from her own doctors."

Lark sank to her knees beside the feverish Sheeda. "There, there, it'll be all right. Barton says so. He wouldn't lie to you. Never. Oh, darling Sheeda, why did this have to happen?"

Kinsolving drew Vandy aside. "Check the scanners and locate Davi Jessarette."

"If Cameron has blanked out himself and Suarez, why not cancel Jessarette from the computer banks, too?"

"Cameron must have a reason, if we can find Jessarette. Whatever it is, you can bet that it's part of a bigger scheme." It did not surprise him when the stocky security agent popped onto the vidscreen.

"That's in an area we're repairing," Vandy said, studying the surroundings. "Every few months we renovate. Suarez might have moved from the underground lab to one of those buildings. Nothing but robot workers would be around. They wouldn't report back unless someone tried to stop them while they worked. Only the supervisor robots have the capability of evaluating if something is amiss outside their programmed area of responsibility."

"Cameron could circumvent them easily enough," said Kinsolving. He worried at the ease in finding Jessarette. What did Cameron have in mind? Did he use Jessarette as bait for a trap? If so, the prey was about to step boldly into the jaws of the trap.

"Bart," spoke up Vandy, "there's something wrong with this. Let me send in a security squad."

He shook his head. "He might not allow it. If Cameron wants me there, then I'll go. But I've got to have an edge, something to insure that he doesn't simply walk away after killing me."

"What is that?" asked Vandy.

Kinsolving had no answer.

"I don't want you coming with me," said Kinsolving. "It's too dangerous."

"Just being supervisor of Paradise has become 'too dangerous,'" said Vandy Azmotega. "Fourteen hundred of my guests are dead and there'll be hell to pay when the news arrives on their respective planets. On the entire planet, only Sheeda and one other Onarian are still alive. Both are closer to dead than alive, too."

Kinsolving pushed that from his mind and tried not to panic. The large villa where Jessarette hid might have been designed for use as a fortress—or a prison. Once inside, there would be no easy escape. Cameron had lured him here. He had to find out why.

"I know the place better than anyone else," she said. "Even if Cameron has complete access to my computer, I know this place better than he ever could. This project has been partly rebuilt according to my verbal orders. No computer-recorded plans."

Kinsolving thought she was lying just to join him. He decided that this was her planet, her responsibility, her need to see justice done.

"How do we get inside without triggering all the alarms?" he asked.

Vandy smiled. "This way. A hole in the wall."

They crawled on their bellies through a low ravine and under a rock fence. Inside Vandy explained, "I was going to divert a stream here, then changed my mind."

Kinsolving caught her arm and squeezed, silently cautioning her against speaking. A shadow passed across a wall. He drew the impact laser and felt naked, even with it in hand. Cameron was expert at hunting and killing. And his robots were even better. What chance did anyone really have against a trained assassin?

Kinsolving saw no other choice. Vandy Azmotega had lost control of Paradise because of Cameron's expertise with computer systems. She could do only those chores he allowed. Communication to the alien worlds had been allowed: Cameron wanted fear to spread. Kinsolving wondered if the Plan depended on the arrival of alien vessels to investigate.

He doubted it. As paranoid as those adherents of the Stellar Death Plan were, they would expect the aliens to nuke the planet. Another way of infecting the alien worlds had already been chosen. Of that Kinsolving was certain.

But Cameron might want to play out his hunter-prey games, with nothing more to be gained than satisfaction from killing Kinsolving. That did not ring true, either. Cameron was efficient and would relish Kinsolving's death, but the Plan came first.

"Barton, look," Vandy whispered urgently. She held another impact laser, clumsily pointing it in the direction of the moving shadow.

"Don't fire yet," said Kinsolving. "There's more to do first. Be sure of your target." He made certain she understood.

He had not counted on a voice pickup microphone being trained on him. His words boomed across the large walled estate. The shadow vanished instantly. Kinsolving swore under his breath. Even these words were picked up and clearly broadcast. He bit his lip and looked around, scanning not only the sky but the ground at his feet. A small lump looked suspicious in the perfectly tended lawn. He fired the impact laser. The greater-than-expected explosion told him he had destroyed the remote sensor that had betrayed him.

The satisfaction he felt at finding Cameron's relay robot was instantly blotted out by a high-energy laser bolt ripping through the air and destroying a portion of the wall behind him. The purple haze from the ionization trail snaked back in the direction of the main house. Whoever had cast the shadow had armed himself with a powerful combat laserifle.

The impact laser in his hand made him feel even more helpless. A tiny pistol against such armament spelled suicide. Kinsolving did the only thing he could do. He attacked.

"Cover me!" he yelled over his shoulder at Vandy. She gasped, then settled down and began firing. The pathetic little bolts nipped at the corner of the house. Kinsolving wanted to guide her firing but could not take the time. He kept his head down and charged. Another bolt turned the dirt at his feet into plasma.

He stumbled and rolled and came to his feet in time to tuck his head between outstretched arms. He crashed through an ornate, decorative window. Amid a shower of stained glass he landed facedown inside the mansion. A silent prayer went out. If Vandy had opted for the more usual plastic panes instead of the colorful and archaic stained glass he would have knocked himself out.

Echoes betrayed the rifle wielder. Kinsolving followed the shadows dancing inside the empty house and waited, holding his breath, hand uncommonly steady. The muzzle of the high-energy laserifle poked around the corner of the door. Kinsolving waited, thumb poised to send out the aiming beam. He hardly knew he exhaled slowly when more of the rifle came around. A hand. A wrist. An arm and shoulder.

His thumb touched the toggle. A cherry red aiming beam found a spot on the rifleman's chest. With the sudden understanding of perfect alignment, Kinsolving pressed the trigger. The variable frequency impact laser fired, working its deadly magic on the victim's torso.

A shrill scream split the silence inside the house. Echoes vanished down long corridors. The heavy laser fell from lifeless fingers as the body toppled forward into full view.

Several seconds passed before Kinsolving moved. He had expected to see Jessarette's blasted body. Or, as a distant hope, to find Cameron's corpse. A woman stretched out prone on the floor. He advanced cautiously and pulled the laserifle away. It still carried a full charge. He hefted it, trying to decide which weapon suited him best. Opting for the laserifle's power, he thrust the impact laser into a pocket.

"Barton," came Vandy's breathless voice from the door, "what happened?"

"I thought I'd shot you by mistake," he said, "but I've never seen this woman before. Is she on Suarez's research team?"

"No, he only had the one assistant." Vandy knelt and lifted the fallen woman's head to study the face. "Familiar. Wait a second." Taking her light wand out, she scanned the slack face. Identification came back instantly. "She's a guest. Gerta Urquhart. From Gamma Tertius 4."

"Let me guess," Kinsolving said in disgust. "She's the other guest who arrived after Cameron did. And her friend is already dead."

"And I thought telepathy was impossible." A faint smile wrinkled the corners of Vandy's lips. "Any other lucky guesses?"

Kinsolving could not make sense of it. He had expected Cameron or Suarez and had run afoul of another IM director's employees.

A sudden sharp sound from upstairs alerted him. He motioned Vandy behind him, then started up the broad, winding marble staircase. The lack of furnishings allowed echoes to race unhindered from one end of the mansion to another and made it difficult to determine the exact source of the sound, but he thought it came from the second floor.

He hoped so. He presented a good target should Cameron decide to use him for target practice. But Kinsolving wondered if the robotics master had such a crass end in store for him. Any of a dozen times would have sufficed to send a single killer robot after him. Cameron seemed content to let this strange play unravel, just as the DNA helices in the aliens had already unraveled.

Shards of broken glass on the hall floor told of recent use of the room beyond. Kinsolving pushed the glossy wood door open with the muzzle of the laserifle and looked inside. A makeshift workbench stretched along the far wall. Strewn around were broken glass test tubes and carrying cases for biologic specimens.

Kinsolving opened the door further. He saw a man hunched over, working frantically at a remote console.

It took all his willpower to keep from pressing the firing toggle on the laserifle. Instead, Kinsolving said, "Move away from the computer, Dr. Suarez. We have much to discuss."

Morgan Suarez spun, a startled look on his face. His mouth opened but no words came out. As if he were a marionette and someone had cut his strings, he simply sat down on the floor, eyes glassy and body slack.

CHAPTER FIFTEEN

"HE'S TRYING TO KILL ME," sobbed Morgan Suarez.

For a few seconds Kinsolving thought the man meant him. Kinsolving's finger tensed on the laserifle's firing toggle, then relaxed only through immense force of will.

"He's trying to steal everything I've done. I hate him!"

"Cameron?" Kinsolving moved into the room and quickly glanced around. The worktables were strewn with broken glassware, as though someone had taken a club to the fragile test tubes and complex test equipment. "Do you mean Cameron's trying to kill you?"

"He wants my discovery. No one else has ever done such fine work on Bizzie physiology. No one else has ever unlocked the secrets of their genetic structure—and he wants it for himself!"

"And all you wanted was to kill a few trillion intelligent beings," raged Kinsolving. He had no sympathy for Suarez.

"You're not with him. You're working for them, for the Bizzies, for the enemy!"

Kinsolving felt Vandy Azmotega move up behind him, her hand resting lightly on his shoulder. "He's crazy," she whispered. "Listen to him. He's turned to vacuum between his ears."

"He was crazy long before Cameron arrived," said Kinsolving.

"He stole it all, and I can't get it back. He's got the process."

Kinsolving stared at the scientist huddling in the corner of the room. Not a flicker of pity went out to the man. Suarez had personally murdered fourteen hundred aliens on Paradise. Anything that happened to him was only justice. But Kinsolving could not imagine insanity as fitting punishment for what this man had unleashed. Suarez hardly knew where he was. Kinsolving wanted him to suffer, to regret every day of continued life, to share in the pain he had created.

"Where is Cameron?" he demanded.

"He took it. He got into my work computer and stole the process information. He knows it all!"

"Here," Kinsolving said, handing the laserifle to Vandy. "Be careful. I want to see if I can't help him remember better." Kinsolving walked in a wide berth away from any potential firing line. Suarez stared at him with fright-widened eyes. No intelligence shone forth from those dark eyes that had once flashed with hate. Kinsolving grabbed Suarez and jerked him to his feet.

"Please, stop him. He's got it all."

"What's Cameron going to do with it?"

"He stole it. They—they're trying to take over. They're trying to keep TR from taking part in the Plan."

"Do you mean Interstellar Materials?"

"Yes, them! Fremont and Villalobos and Cameron. That son of a bitch!" wailed Suarez. "Cameron stole it for them. They want to prevent anyone else from taking part in the Plan. They want it all for themselves!"

"The Stellar Death Plan?"

"The universe! With my discovery, they can have it all. Get it back for me." A cunning look came into the demented, haunted eyes. "Steal it back and I'll reward you generously. Anything you want. Just get back the process files!"

"Where is Cameron?" asked Kinsolving, shoving Suarez back against the wall. "I can't do anything for you unless you tell me."

"He's clever, but I'm a genius. *I* invented the process that unravels their DNA," gibbered Suarez.

Kinsolving slammed Suarez hard against the wall. "Where is he? Tell me."

"Cameron? He took it and is smuggling it off-planet. He wants to get it back to IM on Gamma Tertius 4. He told me, the son of a bitch. He's evil. He took it and went back to—"

Suarez's words were abruptly silenced by the roar of an energy weapon. Kinsolving jerked to one side, his sleeve aflame. He spun around to face Vandy, to shout at her for killing Suarez before he had gotten the information he needed. But Vandy was not in the doorway. He saw her feet through the door—and then nothing but the ugly muzzle of the laserifle filled his sight.

"Good riddance," came Jessarette's shrill, cracked voice. He sounded as crazed as Suarez. "I should have killed you on Almost Paradise. Don't know how you got away then, don't know how you got away from my seeker-killer in the meadow, but you won't get away now!"

Kinsolving dived behind a worktable in time to avoid the laserifle's deadly lance of coherent light. Kinsolving felt the beam slicing through plastic and wood just above him. He wiggled on his belly and came to a kneeling position behind an overturned chair. Fumbling for the impact laser in his pocket, Kinsolving waited for Jessarette to move into the room for the kill.

A heartbeat. Two. A dozen. Davi Jessarette did not appear. Kinsolving wondered if the assassin played a waiting game intended to lure him from behind his pitiful barricade.

"Vandy!" he called. "Are you all right?" No answer. Kinsolving gripped the handle of his weapon so tightly he felt the circulation leaving his fingers. Cold hand on the impact laser, he spun around, put his back to the wall and edged along until he got behind the door. Peering through the crack between door and frame, he saw ony Vandy lying facedown in the hall. Kinsolving listened intently. He heard nothing but the subtle sounds of the mansion: air moving through halls, settling noises, occasional pops and whines from plumbing being reworked.

Barton Kinsolving leaped out from behind the door, legs bent and weight forward. His finger almost depressed the trigger of his impact laser. But he had no target. Jessarette had gone. Kinsolving checked in both directions along the hallway before dropping down beside Vandy. He rolled her onto her back and pressed his fingers into her throat, checking for a pulse. He almost cried with relief when he felt a slow, firm beat in the carotid artery.

Her eyes flickered. She opened her brown eyes. For an instant she looked confused. Then memory rushed back. "Someone hit me!" she cried, trying to sit up. Kinsolving held her down.

"It was Jessarette. He's gone."

"What about Suarez?"

"Jessarette used the laserifle he took from you. He killed him." Kinsolving could not keep the bitterness from his voice. "He killed Suarez before he told me where Cameron had taken the information he stole."

"Cameron's got it?"

"Suarez wasn't too clear but I got the impression that IM sees this as their chance to be number one in everything. They want to kill the aliens and take over their worlds. They also want to prevent others involved in the Plan from gaining."

"A falling out among thieves and murderers. Seems like justice," said Vandy. Kinsolving let her sit up slowly now. The woman's eyes had lost their shocky glaze and she seemed none the worse for the blow to the back of her head. A small spot there still sluggishly oozed blood, but it did not appear to be a serious wound.

"The sides are lining up wrong, though," observed Kinsolving.

"What do you mean?"

"Why would Jessarette kill Suarez? They both worked for TR. It looks as though Jessarette is in league with Cameron." Kinsolving frowned even as he spoke. He had seen the drugged look on Jessarette's face when he had seen the trio together in the underground lab. Jessarette had been under Cameron's control. Later, however, Jessarette seemed free of the robot master's influence. Why should Jessarette want to kill Suarez unless he had gone insane, too?

"Do you think the virus affected them?" asked Vandy, as if reading his mind.

"Possible, but I doubt it. Everything you said about Suarez makes me think he was a meticulous researcher. He would have tried out the unraveling virus on humans before pronouncing it 'safe.'"

"Safe," she scoffed. "He might have created a time bomb for humans. Aliens it kills immediately. Humans might take longer. Days or weeks or even years."

Kinsolving did not think this was true. "A better explanation is that Jessarette wants it all for himself. With Suarez dead, he might think he can recover the details of the process from Cameron and then turn it over to his boss at Terra Recreations."

"Jessarette doesn't have the ability to get it back from Cameron," Vandy said. Together, they wobbled and teetered out the mansion's front way. The grassy lawns surrounding the estate were empty of all human life.

"You're right about that. Where would Cameron go? How would he try to get the data back to Fremont on Gamma Tertius 4?"

"Message packet," answered Vandy.

"Chancy," said Kinsolving. "Cameron would want to take it himself. He would know it arrived, carrying it himself. He'd want to gloat when he turned it over to Chairman Fremont."

"There'd be a promotion in it for him. That might be his way of insuring he gets credit."

Kinsolving thought Vandy had struck on a plausible reason for Cameron taking the information back personally. It fit with everything he knew of the robot master. Cameron was only hired help at IM. Kinsolving wondered if Cameron's ambitions did not soar to greater heights—such as the chairmanship of the company. Such power would give him a base for even greater conquests.

Did Cameron want to rule human-occupied space by economic power and alien space through stark destructive power? Those involved with the Stellar Death Plan thought in those terms. And of them, Cameron was the most ambitious Kinsolving had encountered.

"How often does a shuttle go up to Almost Paradise?" he asked Vandy.

"Whenever anyone wants to leave. We never keep schedules. Our guests dictate policy in the broadest sense. We want only to please."

"He might be gone, then." The emotional letdown Kinsolving felt at this made him sag visibly.

"Not yet. The shuttle had left for the station to pick up a pair of incoming guests. It can't make the return for at least an hour. Possibly longer."

"How can you stop it?"

"Let's get back to my house. All it takes is one simple order. I am, after all, the supervisor on Paradise."

To this, Kinsolving said nothing. After Cameron had

finished reprogramming the Paradise computer, he wondered whether anyone—other than Cameron—would ever be in charge of the resort planet again.

They hurried back, Kinsolving nervously waiting for Jessarette's laserifle blast to cut him in half. Of the TR security man he saw no trace. Kinsolving insisted on entering Vandy's quarters first to check for traps. He found no sign of Jessarette or Cameron's insidious robots.

That worried him more than if the house had been filled with automated booby traps.

"Punch up the schedule on the shuttle. There. Just as I thought." Vandy settled into her chair, light wand in hand. "Three passengers coming in from Almost Paradise instead of two." She frowned and worked through a passenger profile as Kinsolving waited.

"What's wrong?" He saw the expression on her face turn even darker as a swift parade of data marched past on the vidscreen.

"Two people from IM, one from TR. That's the vice president in charge of off-world resorts on the shuttle. My immediate superior. Ivan Denho." She leaned back in the chair, her face bleak. "The only reason he would be here now is that he knows about Suarez."

"You mean, he sent Suarez here." Kinsolving said the words flatly, as a statement of fact and not a question.

"That's the only possible conclusion. I sent a message packet explaining the plague to the chairman, not Denho. It could not have possibly arrived. Won't for weeks. Denho was already in transit."

Kinsolving sighed. Another supporter of the Plan. Another human who wanted all the aliens in the universe slaughtered.

"The shuttle arrives in thirty minutes. I've put a hold on immediate return to orbit. We should meet it when it arrives."

"And?" he asked.

"Denho is here to see the results of Suarez's field test. I want to show him personally. The automedics had put some of the aliens into a freezer. I want to be sure he sees firsthand what he has released."

"That might not shock sense into him," said Kinsolving.

He knew that the men and women involved in the Plan were ruthless in business. For conquest of the galaxy, they could be even more treacherous and unfeeling.

"It's a start. If that doesn't do it, well, I'll think of something." Kinsolving saw the woman touch the impact laser she had tucked into her pocket.

He started to leave for the shuttle port, then stopped. Something gnawed at the fringes of his mind. It finally came into focus. "See if you can find Cameron with your security system." Vandy tried and failed. Kinsolving had not thought she'd succeed. "Try Jessarette."

"He's already at the shuttle port," she said in surprise. "The system still picks him up."

"Cameron wants us to know where he is. Don't ask why. I have no idea."

"Jessarette is hiding at the north end of the landing port. We can get near him by taking an underground service tunnel that goes to the liquid metals supply building."

Kinsolving stared at the vivid, three-dimensional image of Jessarette on the vidscreen, then shook his head. Cameron was luring them into a trap. Or was Jessarette more than bait?

Vandy and Kinsolving hurried to an underground access point, went down and ran along the tunnel, choosing not to take any of the conveyances they found. Neither had any desire to repeat the experience with the bomb aboard the travel cab. Kinsolving thought that Jessarette had been responsible for that clumsy attempt on their lives, but he could never know for certain. Better to travel on foot than to risk Cameron's more subtle destructive skills.

"How much farther?" Kinsolving gasped. While working as a mining engineer on Deepdig, he had stayed in peak physical condition. Since he had arrived on Paradise, he had accumulated injuries to the point where he was one step away from collapse: his back hurt; the burn on his arm from Jessarette's near miss had not been tended and only now began to annoy him. And rest? He could not remember when he had last gotten a good night's sleep or a square meal. For most, this was a pleasure resort. For him it had become an endurance contest.

It was a contest he was losing slowly.

"Here we are," said Vandy. Sweat ran down her face in

salty trails. She did not look in any better shape than he felt. "What's the plan?"

"Cameron seems to want us to stop Jessarette. Why else leave his recognition symbols in the security system? Since we have nothing better to do, we go after Jessarette."

"Cameron wants us to stop Jessarette so he won't have to. Jessarette knows Cameron stole the process to create the unraveling virus. That's got to be it." Vandy sounded satisfied with this reasoning. Kinsolving didn't bother to tell her that Cameron could remove Jessarette easily whenever he wanted. The man was playing a game with them. Cameron could as easily order his armada of robot killers after them. There would be no place in Paradise to hide if he decided on their deaths.

"This comes out behind Jessarette?" he asked.

Vandy nodded. She stared at him for a moment, then impulsively stepped forward and kissed him. "For luck," she said.

Before Kinsolving could speak, the supervisor of Paradise scampered up the ladder and irised open the door leading to the shuttle port. Warm sunlight flooded down the shaft and softly caressed his face. He could almost believe in peace and relaxation and taking a vacation on this serene planet. Almost.

He followed, impact laser in hand. Kinsolving sidled past Vandy and onto the tarmac. One story warehouses dotted the area. Davi Jessarette could be anywhere, waiting.

"What's he waiting for?" Kinsolving asked aloud. "Is he really waiting to kill Cameron or is he waiting for Denho?"

"I didn't know the vice president was coming. How could Jessarette?" Vandy put a hand over her mouth as she spoke. "Oh. He might have known. Denho might have told him that he'd be out to see the field test of the virus."

"Paradise," said Kinsolving, shaking his head. "The planet is more like a hunting preserve. And we have to guess who's being hunted and why and where we can hide to keep from being killed."

"Sounds like an interesting game. And it would be," said Vandy, "if our lives didn't depend on it."

Kinsolving decided on one warehouse as the best observation point. He motioned to Vandy to stay where she was in the safety of the service tunnel entrance.

"Wait, Bart. I've got an idea. What if Cameron isn't the one with the process information?"

"What?" Kinsolving tried to pull his mind from attack-mode and into thinking about what she said. It proved too difficult. "I don't understand what you mean."

"What if Jessarette is the one with the information and Cameron wants us to get it for him?"

"No," he said without conviction. Jessarette might have Suarez's records, but Cameron could get them too easily. Why use Kinsolving and Vandy to kill Jessarette? Unless it amused him?

"He might. This has to be it. Jessarette has Suarez's process and is going to turn it over to Denho when he arrives. Cameron wants it and is going to let us kill Jessarette, then will kill us to get it. He wants us to risk our necks rather than do it himself!"

A tiny movement in a warehouse doorway alerted Kinsolving to the danger ahead. He grabbed Vandy and pulled her along, hoping that Jessarette had not seen them. The deadly lightning bolt from the laserifle that gouged a huge smoking rut in the tarmac convinced him that they had been seen.

"Circle the building," Kinsolving said. "If Jessarette is alone, one of us will be able to get a shot at his back. Don't try for heroics. It's too dangerous. Go on. Do it!" He shoved Vandy around the side of the building, knowing it would take her several minutes to get into position. By then, the fight would be over.

Either he or Davi Jessarette would be dead.

Kinsolving swung around the corner of the building, ready to fight.

CHAPTER SIXTEEN

BARTON KINSOLVING paused for an instant, then entered the warehouse. Hellacious heat boiled in front of him as the door melted. Jessarette's laserifle reduced the metal-clad door to a puddle. Kinsolving brushed off the bits of metal stinging his cheeks and dived forward onto his belly. He landed hard and skidded, impact laser ready.

Wherever Jessarette hid, he gave Kinsolving no target. Kinsolving scrambled to get his feet under him. Another lance of coherent light took the flesh off his back. Kinsolving almost fainted from the agony that lanced into him. Every injury he sustained seemed to be to his back. He collapsed onto his face, grimly hanging on to consciousness.

He watched the red sighting beam bob and bounce closer and closer. At the last instant he heaved himself to one side. The tiny red bead held steady on the spot he had vacated. Concrete exploded when Jessarette triggered the laserifle again.

Kinsolving had no idea how many times Jessarette's power laser weapon could be fired before it needed recharging. The way he felt, it might not need recharging. A simple ion arc might be enough to knock him over. Wincing with the pain, he duck-walked around the perimeter of the warehouse. Automated equipment went about its business, moving crates in and out, finding the provisions asked for by those who ran Paradise and delivering them.

Ignoring the robot workers wasn't as easy as Kinsolving hoped. They worked in every section of the large warehouse, and he jumped in reaction every time one came near.

"You won't be able to get away with this, Jessarette," he called, hoping the man would betray his position. Jessarette did not respond. Kinsolving dropped to his knees and leaned his forehead against a crate, sweat and blood trickling down. He touched the bloody scratch. He had no idea when he had done this—or how. Pain from his back overrode any other sensory message his body sent his brain.

Through it all came the thought that Jessarette had not answered. This was unlike the killer. Jessarette was a braggart, a man who boasted to increase his own minuscule self-esteem.

Kinsolving used the pain as a goad to get himself moving. He burst forward, smashed into the side of the crate and sent a robohandler bleeping in distress. But the sudden exposure did not bring instant death from the laserifle.

Kinsolving cursed. Jessarette had left the warehouse after the last attack. Where had he gone? Kinsolving looked around frantically and finally saw a small inspection window whose frame had been twisted. He ran to it and peered outside.

He went cold inside when he saw Vandy sneaking around the corner.

"Get down!" he shouted. "Jessarette's outside. He—" The rest of his words were drowned out in the sizzling roar of the laserifle firing. He watched Vandy straighten, look down at the fist-sized hole in her chest, then slowly twist to one side. She fell to the tarmac and lay there, not moving.

Kinsolving's gaze traced back along the purpled ionization trail left by the laser beam. He saw the stack of crates being tended by the robohandlers. One side of a plastic crate had bubbled and flowed. Jessarette had rested the heavy laserifle barrel against the crate to steady his aim. The slight dispersion in the barrel had caused the damage.

When a shadow appeared on the ground, Kinsolving raised his impact laser. He had passed emotion. He had become a hollow shell driven only by instinct. Killing Jessarette would not be revenge; it would not be pleasure; it would be a simple act like breathing.

Jessarette poked his head out around the crate. Kinsolving's finger squeezed down on the impact laser's trigger. The high frequency whine had barely died when Kinsolving realized that he had missed. The aiming laser on his weapon had been knocked off target. Even though he had pinpointed Jessarette's temple, the variable-frequency beam had ripped apart the crate beside him.

"Come back here!" Kinsolving screamed. All the emotion he had pushed aside came rushing back. He trembled so hard that he was unable to properly aim the laser using both hands. He fired repeatedly, the shots going wild. One struck a robot cargo handler. Its silvered carapace exploded and sent a rain of molten metal down over the shuttle port. Another blast melted through a cargo case and set fire to the material inside. Huge plumes of heavy black smoke billowed from within. Kinsolving heard alarms sounding in the distance.

Pain wracking his every move, he tumbled through the small window and fell to the tarmac. He got to hands and knees, then struggled to his feet. As if his boots had been dipped in lead, he moved with agonizing slowness toward Vandy Azmotega. She lay on her side. He turned her over and saw the surprised expression on her face. Death had come too quickly for her to appreciate it. For that small boon, Kinsolving was glad.

"You'll die for this, Jessarette," he vowed. "And you, too, Cameron. You, too!" Kinsolving spun and fired his impact laser from the hip. The beam caught an aerial robot and blew it apart so thoroughly that nothing fell to the ground. The robot spy had been reporting back to Cameron, he knew. Kinsolving reached out and braced himself against the building as he scanned the azure sky for sign of other aerial robots.

They were probably somewhere, but he failed to locate them. Sirens came closer. He guessed that it was the firefighting robots racing to extinguish the blaze in the pile of crates. Whatever had been in the crate he had hit ignited the cargo on either side. A minor fire had become major.

Kinsolving slid the impact laser into his pocket, reached down and took Vandy's weapon, then staggered off across the tarmac. The shuttle would not land for a few minutes. He had time. He had to find Jessarette and kill him. Nothing else was in his mind.

He had no idea where he was going. He tried to walk in a straight line in the direction he thought Jessarette had taken, but he came to the shuttle waiting room. Shaken, weak and almost beyond the limits of his endurance, Kinsolving leaned against the building, its cool plastic wall soothing him.

"Barton?" came a tremulous voice. "Is that you? You're a fright!"

"Lark, help me," he said, tumbling into her arms.

Kinsolving never—quite—lost consciousness. He knew she had summoned an automedic and that the diligent robot doctor worked on him for more than ten minutes. And he silently thanked Lark Versalles when she argued with the machine about putting him into a life-coma. It would be the safe course; every bit of programming in the automedic would dictate it.

Lark convinced the machine to wait.

"How are you feeling? You look positively nuked out!"

"You know how to cheer up a patient, don't you?" he said, trying to smile. He managed only a weak grimace. "Why are you here? At the shuttle port?"

"I've got Sheeda's remains," Lark said, her expression turning even more forlorn. "I'm sending it—her—back to Onar. I never heard what their burial customs are. I . . . I didn't have the heart to find out." Tears rolled down Lark's cheeks. For several seconds Kinsolving tried to figure out what was wrong. It finally came to him. Lark's cosmetic dyes had been neutralized. He stared at unaugmented, naturally colored skin.

"You've got to help me," he said. "More than you have already. Jessarette did this. And Cameron has the full process information on how the virus that killed Sheeda was incubated. Cameron will use it on thousands of alien worlds unless we prevent him from getting it back to Gamma Tertius."

"Your back is burned. The automedic said it was a laserifle."

"Jessarette," he gasped out. "Jessarette did this. And he killed Vandy Azmotega."

"Who?"

"The planetary supervisor. We tried to stop Suarez. Jessarette killed him. And he's hunting for Cameron. Only—"

"Barton, darling, please." She pressed a cool finger to his lips. "You're babbling. I don't understand a word of this. If you keep on, nothing I say will stop the automedic from putting you into a life-coma until a hospital automedic can analyze you."

Kinsolving rolled to one elbow and lifted his impact

laser. The automedic moved fast; Kinsolving reacted faster. The laser bolt blew the compact robot apart.

"Why'd you do that?"

"It won't try to put me into a life-coma now. Help me stand up." Lark's arm provided support but no strength. He had to rely on his own inner resources for that. To his surprise, he found it easy to stand without her assistance.

"Paradise is misnamed," said Lark. "Hell is closer."

"When did Sheeda die?"

"An hour ago. She faded more and more and . . . never regained consciousness. The automedic said that her body chemistry had failed. Enzyme levels or something. I didn't understand."

"The plague works on alien DNA. Cameron knows how to duplicate the virus. Because of the Plan, he'll destroy every alien in the galaxy."

"I don't want any part of this, Bart. Please. Try to understand." Lark cried openly. "Sheeda was more than a friend. I . . . I loved her. We had only known each other for a short time, but it was real, Barton. It was *real*."

He hugged her close and let her cry. The hollow feeling had passed entirely. Replacing it was a burning emotion that threatened to consume him even as it gave him strength.

"There'll be others like Sheeda to die," he said. "Cameron murdered fourteen hundred aliens on Paradise—and it was only a test. He must not be allowed to use the virus on other worlds. Billions more will die. Help me to stop him, Lark. I need you." He held her even closer.

"All right, Barton. But how? What can we do? He has robots that came out of nowhere. You know how lucky we were on GT4 to escape him."

"I know. But we've got to keep trying. He won't give up. We can't do any less."

Kinsolving's mind slipped into a strange state. Solutions rose and died with increasing speed. Only one came with lucid conviction. "Cameron is playing with me. He wants me to kill Jessarette for his amusement. I'll kill him, but it won't be for Cameron. It's going to be for *me*."

And for Vandy, he silently added. She deserved better than a laserifle blast.

"Who is this Jessarette?" asked Lark. Kinsolving quickly explained all that had happened starting with their brief stay on Almost Paradise. Lark fought to believe him. Kinsolving didn't care whether she believed him or not. All that counted was her helping him.

"I think Jessarette is a creature of habit. He isn't clever enough to change his pattern. After killing Vandy he'll look for a place where he feels safe."

"Where's that?"

"We can find out where his quarters are." Kinsolving and Lark left the shuttle port waiting room, Lark glancing back at the small shipping coffin containing Sheeda's cremated remains. Then her attention was fully on the task.

She brightened and said, "I never knew how dull life was before you came along, Bart, darling. There's a certain . . . thrill . . . to all this, isn't there?"

He had to admit that she was right. On Deepdig he had done his job well, had loved Ala Markken and had been in a rut without knowing it. Nothing new happened. He had no future except more mining projects. Now he had a mission, a purpose transcending all others. With or without their help, he had to save most of the intelligent beings in the known galaxy. The impossibility of the project forced him to rise above his personal limitations.

And in so rising, he triumphed where he should have failed.

"There," he said, walking even more briskly. "That's Vandy's house."

"A supervisor on Paradise lives in a hovel?" Lark's shock matched his own surprise when he had seen the simple quarters. He pushed inside and found the light wand Vandy had discarded. He aimed it at the vidscreen and began working through the data he ordered using her executive computer authorizations.

"There's Jessarette's house. Down by the shore."

"That's not five hundred meters from here," said Lark. "Are you sure you want to do this?"

Kinsolving was already out the door, forcing Lark to make a dash to catch up with him. "I want him. He's part of everything that's ugly on Paradise. Jessarette's only a henchman, but he's responsible."

"Barton, wait, please," gasped out Lark. "A question

first. Why don't we use a cab to go there? He wouldn't know it was us. My feet are tired!"

He explained the problems he had experienced with the local transportation. Even as he spoke, Kinsolving looked up into the blue, blue sky for some sign that the shuttle from Almost Paradise was coming in for a landing. He saw nothing, but he picked up the pace until Lark ran to keep even with him. He had to finish dealing with Davi Jessarette in time to meet the shuttle.

Another adherent to the Stellar Death Plan would be aboard: Ivan Denho, vice president of Terra Recreations and as cold-blooded a murderer as any on Paradise.

"It looks so peaceful," Lark said, stopping on a cliff overlooking the ocean. Whitecaps crested on the gentle surf as the water lapped against the pure sand of the beach. "I can't believe such venom has come from this world."

Kinsolving grabbed her in his arms and knocked Lark flat in time to prevent a half dozen laser beams from slicing her into bloody pieces.

"Automatic weapons," he whispered. "Jessarette won't be content to rely on them. He'll have to come out to check." Kinsolving rolled onto his back and experienced a small twinge. The automedic had deadened the pain well this time.

He used his impact laser on rock outcroppings. Repeatedly firing, he exposed the sensors Jessarette had planted to monitor anyone approaching his secluded dwelling. Then Kinsolving began work on the laser traps themselves. In less than five minutes he had produced a dozen minor explosions.

"That ought to take care of Jessarette's defenses," he said smugly.

"What now?" asked Lark.

"We wait for him to get nervous." But it was Kinsolving who got tired of waiting. He did not want Jessarette slipping out by a hidden escape route.

Kinsolving motioned for Lark to be silent, then moaned in mock agony. Louder, he called out, "Damn you, Jessarette. Those lasers of yours cut off my legs. The shock's wearing off. The pain's too much! I'm going to die!"

Kinsolving gripped his impact laser so tightly he felt the

tingling of lost circulation. He relaxed. He had to be precise. There might be only one shot at Jessarette when he came to personally kill his victim.

Kinsolving waited—and grew more impatient. Jessarette did not rise to the bait.

Lark Versalles moved so unexpectedly that Kinsolving could do nothing to stop her. The woman stood upright, blond hair gleaming like gold in the sun, the other colors in her hair making her stand out even more. She cried, "Barton, darling, don't die! I'll help you!"

A dislodged rock warned Kinsolving in time. He had been watching the front entrance to Jessarette's house. A portion of a boulder ten meters to the side swung open to reveal a passage drilled through solid rock. Jessarette had stepped out and turned his ankle on a loose stone. This noise brought Kinsolving's impact laser about.

He fired and missed.

Jessarette yelped in surprise and tried to retreat. Kinsolving held the trigger of his laser down discharging it completely. The vibratory beam struck the rock in front of Jessarette and blew the boulder apart, cutting off his passage. The killer spun, heavy laserifle in his hand. His lips pulled back in a snarl. "I got you now, Kinsolving. That drained your laser."

Kinsolving reached into his pocket and withdrew the laser he had used in the warehouse. He silently reminded himself that the aiming beam was off. He corrected for this. Then he stood.

"Bart," gasped Lark. "He's got a *rifle!*"

Davi Jessarette's face lit with triumph. He had a laserifle. But Barton Kinsolving had justice on his side. The bolt from the impact laser removed Jessarette's head from his shoulders.

Kinsolving stared at the headless corpse and said, "You should have suffered more."

The thunderclap rolling across the ocean drew his attention skyward. The shuttle glowed a cherry red as it slipped through the heavy atmosphere of Paradise on its way to a landing at the port.

"Come on, Lark," he said. "We've got more to do.

We've got to stop Cameron from leaving with the information on the virus."

Kinsolving slowed only long enough to scoop up the fallen laserifle. He knew he would need it later.

CHAPTER SEVENTEEN

BARTON KINSOLVING reached the shuttle port in no condition to do anything more strenuous than sit on the ground and gasp for breath. Lark Versalles stood over him, glowering. "You should have let me pick out a cab. We could have been here in half the time with no effort. Sometimes I wonder about you, Bart."

"The bomb," he said, knowing how silly this sounded now. Davi Jessarette was dead. The other woman sent by Interstellar Materials was dead. Only Cameron remained —and why would the robot master choose a crude bomb when his sophisticated, almost undetectable robot killers would be more suitable? Kinsolving cursed his stubborness. He and Vandy had almost been blown up. The thought stuck in his mind and refused to go away.

For all the good saving her had done, he thought with real bitterness. He tried to come up with substantive accomplishments and failed. Sheeda was dead, along with fourteen hundred aliens. The test for the Stellar Death Plan had been successful. Cameron had stolen the genetic blueprint for the engineered virus and had seen to removing Morgan Suarez. As surely as if he had lasered the scientist, Cameron had killed him, Kinsolving knew. Davi Jessarette had been a pawn and nothing more.

"The shuttle's down," said Lark. "Who is it you want to stop?"

"Ivan Denho, a vice president for TR. And I think he's here to carry the genetic map for the virus back with him to Earth."

"Why?" asked Lark.

"What? So he can finish what they've started. Mass produce the virus, release it, kill the aliens. You know that."

Lark shook her head and sent a soft cascade of hair falling into her eyes. She brushed it away with an impatient gesture. "You said Cameron wanted it for himself. Why turn it over to TR? They probably think it's theirs since Dr. Suarez was their researcher, but why would Cameron suddenly cooperate?"

"He has to get it off planet and knows we're waiting," Kinsolving said, more to himself than to Lark. Everything the woman said made sense. Cameron had put himself into competition with TR. Denho arrived, knowing nothing of the power play being acted out. Kinsolving's mind worked through what it would be like when Cameron met Denho.

"Cameron goes up the corporate ladder if IM controls the plague, not TR," he said.

In a way he and Denho were working for the same goal: to prevent Cameron from getting the information off-planet. The difference lay in what would be done with the information should either get it.

Denho would use it. Kinsolving would destroy it.

"Destroy it," he said aloud. "We've got to get the information away from Cameron and destroy it."

Lark looked at him, annoyance written on her face. "Barton, darling, are you all right? That's *silly*. Really a vacuum thing to say. Nature is a blabbermouth. What Dr. Suarez discovered, someone else can duplicate. You can't think that TR doesn't have others who know what he was trying to do."

Kinsolving sat and shook all over. His body hurt, his temples throbbed with the beginning of a massive headache, and he found it harder to keep a logical train of thought moving along. Lark was right. Simply destroying the information would do nothing to prevent others from working on it.

"What else can we do?" he said numbly.

"Get the bioweapon from Cameron and turn it over to the aliens. Let them see what's been done. They've got labs of their own, I suppose. They can develop a vaccine for it."

"That's a good idea, Lark." Kinsolving painfully worked to his feet and leaned against her. "I'm glad you're helping me. I really am."

"You look worse than ever," she said, eyeing him critically. "Pale. Your hands shake. You can barely walk. What good are you going to be against this Denho—or Cameron?"

Kinsolving did not answer. His mind slipped into its more usual channels of clarity. "What do we need Denho for?" he asked. "Cameron isn't going to give him the bioweapon. Denho is here thinking he'll meet Suarez."

Lark and Kinsolving exchanged glances. They both smiled broadly. "So we tell him all about Cameron," they said in unison.

Excited now, Kinsolving went on. "Let Denho do the work for us. Let him track down Cameron and get the information. Then we take it from *him*."

"We're making a big assumption," said Lark. "How good is this Denho? Good enough to best Cameron?"

Kinsolving shrugged. They could only hope that Terra Recreations did not promote idiots to the rank of vice president.

"Here," said Lark. She had motioned over a small flatbed cargo loader. "We ride out to the shuttle. No more walking. I'm tired; you're *exhausted*."

Kinsolving climbed onto the cargo platform. Everything Lark said was true.

He pointed when he saw a low-slung cab leaving the shuttle. "Are we too late? There're two people inside."

"There's a guy leaving the shuttle who looks like his name ought to be Ivan Denho." Lark gave an involuntary shiver and snuggled closer, her arm circling Kinsolving's waist.

The man waiting impatiently on the tarmac did look as though his name would be Ivan Denho. Shaped like a fleshy bullet, his shaved head gleamed in the bright sunlight. Thick arms threatened to split the sleeves of a conservative royal purple and pastel pink business suit. His bulk made him appear fat; Kinsolving saw no evidence of that in the man's quick, precise movements. Strength and a quick reaction time lay under that brutish exterior.

"Someone broke his nose," Lark said with some distaste. "Why didn't he get it fixed? And made smaller—it looks like a fat potato all mashed over his face."

"Our Mr. Denho is obviously a man who cares little for appearance." Kinsolving had seen this type of executive before. All that mattered was action, accomplishment, results.

Kinsolving thought that Denho might stand a chance against Cameron. He had feared that TR's vice president might be some office-bred bureaucratic lackey who had advanced by saying "yes" to the right people often enough.

If anything, Ivan Denho had fought his way to his present position.

"What should we do?" asked Lark. "We've got to think of something. We're almost there."

Kinsolving tried to formulate a clever plan that would give him exactly what he wanted, but exhaustion again claimed him. His thoughts jumbled and he failed to decide anything workable.

Denho settled the matter for him. The man shouted and waved a pudgy hand, summoning them over. Lark ordered the cargo transport to the shuttle.

"You two, I need immediate transportation to Supervisor Azmotega's office."

"Climb aboard, sir," said Kinsolving. "Nothing fancy, but it'll get us there."

Denho hopped onto the platform and sat down, not caring that he dirtied his expensive suit. The man's dark eyes peered from under heavy bony ridges. Nothing moving across the tarmac escaped his notice. "What the hell's wrong with this place?" he asked. "Supervisor Azmotega is more capable than this operation appears." Denho turned and scowled at Kinsolving.

"Nothing's been right lately, sir," said Kinsolving. "Plague. Killed all the aliens on Paradise."

Denho jerked as if Kinsolving had touched him with an electric wire. "How do you know that?"

"Hard to stack that many bodies without someone noticing and commenting."

"Do the human guests know?"

Denho had mistaken Kinsolving for a common worker. Kinsolving hoped that the man did not look too closely at Lark. Even without her expensive cosmetic dyes activated, it would be difficult to believe that she was anything but a customer on Paradise.

"No," answered Kinsolving. "But there's more than a few thousand deaths on Paradise," he said. "The supervisor is dead. She was killed when a... security agent went crazy. Must have been from the plague." Kinsolving saw no reason not to sow the seeds of uneasiness concerning the plague in Denho's mind.

"What are you saying?" the man demanded. His attention focused fully on Kinsolving. Kinsolving felt as if he had become a specimen under an electron microscope. The only relief he felt from this was that Denho completely ignored Lark.

"Davi Jessarette," explained Kinsolving. "He murdered her."

"Jessarette?"

"None other," said Kinsolving. "Rumor has it that he and an Interstellar Materials employee named Cameron did it. Some dispute over money, maybe."

Denho's face lost all expression, but Kinsolving saw the new hardness come into the man's already flinty eyes. He did not need to tell the TR vice president anything more about the deaths. Denho had figured it all out in a flash.

"Take me to this Cameron," Denho ordered.

Kinsolving shook his head. "Can't. Don't know where he is. Supervisor's dead. Only she had access to the computers. You know any way of finding him?" Kinsolving did not want to appear too knowledgeable by telling Denho of the planetary computer's malfunction—of Cameron's reprogramming.

"Take me to Supervisor Azmotega's office."

Kinsolving motioned. Lark altered the direction of travel slightly. They cruised back to Vandy's house in a fraction of the time they'd taken getting to the shuttle port. When they arrived Denho slipped off and stalked into the house without uttering a word.

Lark watched his broad back vanish inside. Only then did she speak. "Should we spy on him?"

"Why not?" Kinsolving and Lark went to the still open door and peered inside. Denho reached into his pocket and drew out a light wand similar to Vandy's. To Kinsolving's surprise, Denho was successful in using it to locate Cameron.

"It worked," he muttered to Lark. "That means either Denho had access to a deeper level in the computer than Vandy or that Cameron wants him to find him."

"You two, take me to these coordinates." Denho barked the numbers. Kinsolving had no idea where it was. Lark punched the numbers into the cargo loader's navigation computer and they started off. Kinsolving started to ask Denho more about locating Cameron, then subsided. Denho sat, powerful arms crossed, his face a mask. He radiated the message: Leave me alone.

To Kinsolving's surprise, the coordinates turned out to be the mansion being renovated where Suarez had been killed. The loader platform came to a halt at the foot of a path. Denho hopped off. He made a brusque motion of dismissal. "That'll be all."

"You need a security team, sir?" asked Kinsolving.

His only answer was a grunt and watching Denho's broad shoulders vanish through the door. Ivan Denho was a man of few words.

"What now?" asked Lark.

"We've been dismissed. I suppose we can take a break." Kinsolving reached under the pile of rags in the cargo bed and drew out the laserifle he had taken from Jessarette.

"Inside?"

"Where else," he said, smiling. He had been able to rest enough to regain strength. With Lark a step behind him, Kinsolving went to a window and peered inside the abandoned mansion. Since he had been here a few hours earlier, robot workers had stripped the walls and had begun to install new electronics equipment. Kinsolving couldn't begin to understand what this room would be used for when they finished.

His only interest lay in Denho. The squat, bald man stood stolidly in the center of the room, studying his wrist chronometer. From the faint blue glow, Kinsolving guessed that it told more than the local time. Denho moved slowly in a circle until he was satisfied with the readings given by his sensors.

He walked to the stairs leading to the room where Suarez had died. Denho paused, drew out a weapon unfamiliar to Kinsolving, then started up.

"What do we do now? Wait?" asked Lark.

"There's nothing upstairs. I looked through the room where Suarez had his lab. He was trying to get the data he needed from his computer, but Cameron had already erased it." Kinsolving glanced back over his shoulder, an eerie sense of being watched making him increasingly uneasy. He saw nothing, but Cameron's robots could be anywhere. Although he did not know, he thought they might even be high in the air looking down. Their size made them impossible to see if they were more than a few hundred meters above.

"Here's a door into the lower levels," said Lark, peering into the darkened stairway leading down.

"Cameron's down there," Kinsolving said with sudden conviction. "Don't ask me how I know. It just feels right."

He hurried down the stairs and found the door securely locked. He used the laserifle on it, sending molten fragments back into his face and across his chest.

"Barton, be careful," chided Lark. "You'll set us both on fire, doing things like that."

Kinsolving ignored her protest. He hurried inside, knowing that the roar of the rifle would have alerted Denho. Kinsolving stopped and lifted the laserifle, triggering it repeatedly when he saw small movements at the edges of his field of vision. Tiny explosions marked each robot he destroyed.

"The robots!" cried Lark. "Cameron *is* here!"

Kinsolving rushed forward, laserifle swinging to and fro, ready for instant use. He had to use it on several larger robots.

Then he met one machine too heavily armored to be stopped by the potent energies released by the weapon he carried.

"It's like a tiny war tank!" warned Lark. She huddled down behind Kinsolving.

He motioned her back. "Cameron's still here. Denho found him—or Cameron wanted Denho to find him." His next words were drowned out by the throaty roar from the robot's laser cannon. The entire corridor exploded in flame. Kinsolving was protected by a shallow doorway but quickly found this was not enough. The superheated air rushed out the open doorway—and along with it went his breath.

Gasping for air in the vacuum caused by the miniature firestorm, Kinsolving fell to his knees.

More from reaction than thought, he fired his laserifle.

It blew a deep hole in the floor in front of the robot tank. For a split second, the tank rumbled forward and fell laser muzzle first into the hole. Kinsolving aimed this time and raked the laserifle's beam of coherent light over the top of the robot.

"You killed it," marvelled Lark, when she saw the machine struggled to right itself and failed. "It can't get out."

"I just wounded it," said Kinsolving, thinking of the robot as a living creature, too. "But now it dies." He had damaged the right track system. He melted it off with a dozen more bolts. Then he began blasting at the left side. Even after absorbing enough energy to kill a thousand men, the robot struggled to come after him.

It proved a futile effort on the machine's part. It only succeeded in burrowing deeper into the glassy grave Kinsolving had blasted for it in the floor.

Kinsolving motioned for Lark to edge past the still fighting robot. He spun and burst into a room. Empty. The next proved equally as deserted. The third, however, had a stairway leading upward. He caught a momentary flash of flame-orange and gray fabric.

"Cameron!" he shouted. "Get back here and fight!"

He lasered four robots who answered his challenge. But their master had vanished up the stairs.

"Barton, whatever was here is gone," said Lark. She pointed to a small computer. Its block memory had been removed. "Cameron took the permanent memory with him."

Kinsolving turned to follow Cameron, then stopped. He went across the littered floor to the small computer unit and stared at it. "Find me another block circuit. There must be one around somewhere."

"Here," Lark said. "But it's empty. Blank. Cameron's got the one with Dr. Suarez's bioweapon plans on it."

"You're right when you said that Cameron took the permanent memory. But the computer is still on. The transient memory might still contain the information we want if Cameron was examining it when we burst in on him."

"What good does that—oh!" she exclaimed. "If it's still in transient, you can read it off to a permanent block as long as the power hasn't been turned off!"

"It's worth a try." Kinsolving inserted the blank circuit,

then began to work on the console. A broad smile grew until it was almost painful. Complex diagrams of DNA helices began to appear on screen. Following this came a detailed description of how to incubate the genetically engineered virus.

"Are you recording it?" Lark asked anxiously.

"All of it. There!" Kinsolving snatched the block circuit from the computer and tucked the slim ceramic cartridge into his pocket. "Now we can find Cameron."

He started up the stairs slowly, laserifle ready for anything. Kinsolving would not let Cameron escape. He wouldn't!

CHAPTER EIGHTEEN

BARTON KINSOLVING fired at the robots moving toward him, even though they did not seem menacing. He had seen Cameron's craft too often to take chances. The robots *popped!* out of existence. He peered cautiously into the room at the head of the spiral staircase from the cellar. Work robots labored to renovate the mansion. He saw the eye-dazzling combinations, the optical effects that turned the room into one a thousand times bigger, the tricks and decorations and programming of robots paramount.

Of Cameron he saw nothing.

"What's happening, Barton?" whispered Lark.

"He's vanished. I don't see him anywhere."

"Did you hear a door closing?"

"No," Kinsolving said. "But that doesn't mean he's still inside. There are other ways outside. A window might have been open—the work robots are tearing out walls everywhere."

"He's still inside," Lark said firmly. "I feel it."

Kinsolving did, too. Cameron had a chance to flee and had not taken it. Why? A trap? Possibly. Kinsolving had a gut level feeling that it was more. Cameron had been surprised in the cellar. The residual memory in the computer proved that. Cameron's usual thoroughness would have made him erase the transient memory if he had not been interrupted.

A pair of scintillant points came wobbling into the room, orbiting around one another. Bright blue sparks shot from the tiny points of pure energy, setting fires wherever they touched. Two safety robots trailed behind, putting out the incipient blazes.

"What are those?" Kinsolving wondered aloud. He raised his laserifle but did not fire.

"I've never seen anything like them," said Lark, standing on tiptoe and peering over his shoulder. "They don't look friendly."

"They don't look like robots," Kinsolving said.

"That doesn't mean Cameron didn't send them after us."

Even as the woman spoke, the brilliant specks revolved around and aligned in such a fashion that one was hidden behind the other during part of the orbit.

Kinsolving fired at the same instant that the hidden speck blossomed and grew into a blinding flower of light. The shock wave knocked him back into Lark. Her arms wrapped around Kinsolving's body for support, the pair tumbled back down the spiral staircase to the cellar.

"Are you all right, Bart, darling?"

"Blinded. No, just temporarily blinded. All I can see are blue and yellow dots." He closed his eyes and when he opened them in a few seconds, vision had returned. Tears streamed down his cheeks and small blisters popped up on his face.

Lark took the laserifle from his hands and pointed it upward. He started to tell her that she didn't have her finger on the firing toggle when the remaining spark appeared at the top of the stairs. As though blind and cautiously descending, the dancing spirits came downward, following the stairs rather than floating directly into the cellar.

"Don't shoot," Kinsolving said. "I think that's what blinded me."

"I don't want it touching me," Lark said in distress. She cowered from the bobbing mote of pure energy. It followed her movement.

"It's tracking you," Kinsolving said. "Don't move. Let it come closer. It's some type of free-floating plasma."

"It's getting closer!" she shrieked. "Don't let it hurt me, Barton!"

Kinsolving waved his arms. The speck stopped in its inexorable pursuit of Lark and seemed to home in on him.

"It's not motion sensitive. I think it follows air movement. Maybe we generate positive ions when we move. It acts as though it is being drawn electrically." Kinsolving moved his right hand to the side. The speck curved in its path to mimic his every movement.

"Do something!"

Kinsolving acted without thinking. He sprinted for the far side of the cellar. As if imbuing new life into the scintillant spark, this sudden movement brought it after him almost faster than vision could track. Kinsolving dived behind Cameron's discarded computer console.

The explosion just centimeters above him blew him facedown into the floor. He shook off bits of burning plastic and cracked ceramic vidscreen from his back and stood.

"It destroyed the computer," Lark said in a low monotone, as if in shock.

"It came after me but it couldn't change direction fast enough to avoid hitting the computer. Everything shorted out. The drop of ball lightning discharged itself along the computer's ground wires."

"How did Cameron . . ."

"Not Cameron's," Kinsolving said with conviction. "This must be something put into the fight by Denho." He remembered the man's confidence in confronting Cameron. Even if he did not know of Cameron's expertise with robots, Denho had to guess that he faced a trained killer possibly responsible for Vandy Azmotega's death. Ivan Denho had not hesitated. To Kinsolving this meant that the TR executive carried enough weaponry to win any battle.

Kinsolving motioned for Lark to go back through the cellar and outside. Going back up the stairs to the rooms above only gave Cameron and Denho a second chance to waylay them. Exiting onto the broad, grassy lawn beside the mansion, Kinsolving exercised caution.

"There!" cried Lark. "Going into the woods. Two men."

Kinsolving had seen the bright splash of Cameron's jacket. Of Denho he had seen nothing, but he did not dispute Lark's word. She had been looking directly into the small stand of low-limbed trees while he checked the front of the mansion.

He tried to decide between pursuing the pair and just letting them kill each other. Kinsolving's mind raced. He came to a decision. It seemed more like justice if Denho and Cameron died by his hand. Kinsolving started after them.

"Barton, wait," called Lark. She hung back. "Don't.

Let them go. You have the block circuit with the information about the plague. All you have to do is get it to an alien official."

"I can't give up on Cameron. I just can't." He tried to make her understand, but he wasn't sure that he understood his own motivations. Cameron and the others had used him as a pawn in their treacherous schemes. He had it within his power to fight back, and he was going to do it.

He had to!

Kinsolving heard a distant roar and looked up into the sky. A pinpoint of orange and blue appeared, grew larger, more distinct. The form of a ship all too familiar shone in the bright Paradise sun.

"What is it, Bart?" asked Lark, following his upward gaze.

"A ship landing. From the silhouette, it looks like a Lorr ship."

"They couldn't be after you. They don't know you're here. They can't! We lost them in the Zeta Orgo system."

Kinsolving wondered if Cameron had access to a message packet. Vandy had claimed that she held the reins of power on Paradise, but she had died. Cameron might have sent for the Lorr.

The aliens' presence made it all the more imperative for him to kill Cameron. He might not have another chance.

"Here," he said, thrusting the computer memory block at Lark. "Make sure that this is given to the Lorr. Tell them it's an analysis done by Suarez, that he tried to stop the plague. Lie."

"But, Barton..."

"I've seen firsthand that the aliens won't believe that any human is capable of formulating anything as diabolical—and successful—as the Stellar Death Plan. Try to convince them of the danger facing them, but don't strain their credulity." Kinsolving paused, stared deeply into Lark's fathomless eyes, bent and kissed her, then went hunting for Cameron and Denho.

He didn't care for trophies, but he wanted proof that they would never again menace any living being in the galaxy.

"Barton!" Lark Versalles called after him. Kinsolving

forced himself to keep running and not look back. His resolve might have faded if he caught sight of Lark.

He plunged into the forest and found it denser than it looked from the mansion. Kinsolving slowed, then stopped. He cocked his head to one side and listened intently. After several seconds, he heard movement to his left. He brought up the laserifle and waited.

A small robot shot through the limbs, rustling the leaves as it went. Kinsolving jerked on the laserifle trigger and set fire to both leaves and the robot. It spun in a circle and crashed, causing a new fire. Kinsolving did not try to put it out. He bent double and hurried deeper into the forest, seeking out the man who had sent the robot killer.

In spite of his care, Kinsolving crashed into Denho. The pair recoiled and backed off, facing each other. Kinsolving had the upper hand; the laserifle pointed squarely at Denho's bulky midriff.

"Who are you?" the Terra Recreations vice president demanded. "You're not some simpleton worker, are you?"

"I want Cameron."

"Cameron? Is that the son of a bitch I'm chasing?"

"He has the block circuit with the data on incubating the plague virus. He must not get it off-planet," Kinsolving said.

"You're the one." Denho frowned, his forehead wrinkling all the way to the top of his skull. "The home office had warned me about you. We circulated an alert after the Lorr gave us a photo. You used to work for IM?"

"I can't let anyone involved with the Plan have the memory block Cameron's carrying."

"But, man, they're trying to stifle us!" protested Denho. "The Bizzies cut off our trade, they restrict our exploration, they treat us as inferior beings!"

Kinsolving wondered which of those reasons bothered Denho enough that he would slaughter trillions. He guessed that it was pride, of being considered less than intelligent. Ego drove men like Denho.

"But you don't believe that," Denho went on. "You believe the space dust they teach in the universities on Earth. We'll never *win* the Bizzies' respect. But we can *take* it."

Tiredness, an unwillingness to kill wantonly, misdirection—Kinsolving did not know which betrayed him. Denho had lulled him. The bulky man had reached inside his jacket and had withdrawn a small silver cylinder. From its tip sprang another of the plasma trackers.

"Shoot and we'll both be killed," Denho warned. He began backing off. "It will release enough energy to fry everything within ten meters."

"If I don't, you'll get away."

"You want Cameron dead. I'll kill him for you."

"And release the plague on a thousand worlds!"

Denho's ugly laughter sparked Kinsolving's resolve. His finger lightly flicked the laserifle's trigger, discharging only a tiny amount of energy. The speck of plasma homed in on the ionization trail—but Kinsolving had kept moving. He smashed into a tree trunk, spun around and dived behind a fallen limb. The explosion seared his already wounded back, but he survived.

Kinsolving poked his head up and saw that Denho had taken cover in time to avoid the plasma tracker's detonation. This time he showed no mercy. He leveled the laser and fired.

Denho was outlined in actinic glow—but he did not die. Through the shimmering curtain of energy Kinsolving saw Denho working at controls inside his jacket. He wore a protective field that captured the full energy of the laser, stored it and dissipated the potent charge gradually.

Kinsolving fired again, then attacked, head low and laserifle swinging like a club. He put all his strength into the blow and landed the laserifle barrel on the side of Denho's knee. Kinsolving felt a yielding and heard a loud snapping sound. An instant later Denho screamed in agony and toppled to the ground.

He clutched his injured leg. This gave Kinsolving the chance he needed.

Again Kinsolving swung the heavy laserifle's barrel. It crushed the side of Denho's skull. Blood and torn flesh clung to the laser weapon's barrel. Kinsolving staggered back and leaned against a tree. He had killed before, but he could never make a living out of it. Each death diminished him, turned him inside out and made him sick to his stomach.

"Very well done, Supervisor Kinsolving," came Cameron's mocking voice. "You exceed my projections on your ability every time. I must reconsider the programming on your personality parameters. Underestimating an opponent is dangerous."

"Damn you, Cameron. Where are you?" Kinsolving swung the laserifle around and centered it on the spot where he thought Cameron's voice emanated. He fired. The small *pop!* told of a relay robot's death—but not Cameron's.

"A pity you had to do that. I have only a few of that model of remote left." A deriding laugh infuriated Kinsolving. Then he forced himself to be calm. Cameron goaded him into mistakes. "Yes," Cameron went on, "you have shown great resourcefulness. A pity you do not believe in the goals of the Plan."

Kinsolving began stalking, listening for movement in the forest that might betray Cameron's position.

"You have given me great sport. For that, I must commend you. I had considered killing Jessarette myself. Such a boorish person. But no, I told myself, enjoy the spectacle of Jessarette and Kinsolving stalking each other."

"He killed Vandy Azmotega. You're as responsible for her death as if you strangled her with your own hands."

"Do I detect more than simple anguish over the death of a fellow human? Can it be love you feel for her?"

Kinsolving moved away from the sound of Cameron's voice, then began to circle. He pushed through a curtain of vines and saw the purple and gray of the man's jacket. The laserifle blast had destroyed the last of Cameron's relay robots. The man himself spoke, trying to dupe Kinsolving into thinking it was still being relayed.

But Kinsolving hesitated. He could not see Cameron's face clearly. This might be another ruse, a more elaborate trap set by the cunning robot master.

"I enjoyed watching as you were moved about as if you were one of my mechanical friends," Cameron said. "Jessarette, Denho, both were annoyances. You performed well, supervisor. Now it is time for you to die."

The way the gaudy jacket moved showed a real human inside. Kinsolving thrust his laserifle through the vines and aimed, the sighting beam squarely on the middle of the jacket.

Before his finger tightened and sent a beam of coherent

light death into Cameron's back, Kinsolving heard a rustling sound to his right. He chanced a quick look.

Standing in the brush, a gray-complected Lorr raised a peculiar looking pistol and aimed it at him. Kinsolving let out a yell, pulled the trigger of his own rifle and saw the sighting beam jerk off target. Cameron screamed at the nearness of the deadly beam—but he continued screaming in pain. Kinsolving had not killed him.

A powerful fist crashed into Kinsolving's body, sending him reeling. He landed and shook his head to clear it. No one had been close enough to strike him. He realized, through the haze of pain masking his body, that the Lorr had fired his weapon.

"Halt, human one," came the Lorr's command. "You are the fugitive Barton Kinsolving. I arrest you for—"

The alien's words were drowned out when Kinsolving swung his rifle around and fired. Dry leaves ignited. A curtain of flame shot upward. Kinsolving marvelled at his luck. He had been aiming at the Lorr, not the ground. This worked even better for his purposes. He had no desire to kill the alien, but he wasn't going to be arrested.

Not while Cameron still lived. Not while others of his kind worked for the Stellar Death Plan.

Using the barrier of flames and the resulting black smoke as a shield, Kinsolving rolled to his hands and knees and painfully got to his feet. Not a muscle in his body failed to protest. His back had been burned. His bones hurt from the impact of the Lorr force weapon. But determination carried him onward.

He had almost killed Cameron. Almost. The next time would be his triumph!

Kinsolving stumbled through the vines and into the small clearing where Cameron had been. Kinsolving found tracks in soft dirt leading to the left. Bits of charred cloth marked the path better than the footprints. Behind him he heard the Lorr calling out in his own language, possibly summoning others.

Kinsolving cursed the Lorr police and their efficiency. They had not wasted an instant at the shuttle port. He only hoped that Lark had been successful in convincing someone of importance in the Lorr force that the viral plague posed immense danger to their worlds.

His finger tightened on the trigger when he saw a pair of small robots wiggling along the ground. He vaporized both of them.

"You're running out of machines to protect you, Cameron," he shouted. "I'm going to kill you. You'll never be able to spread that virus on other worlds. The secret will die with you."

Kinsolving lasered through a low shrub and stumbled into the bramble beyond. He ignored the stinging cuts he sustained on his lower legs. Cameron stood stock-still and the aiming beam pointed directly at his chest.

"You've ruined my jacket," the assassin said in an aggrieved voice. "I had it imported from Earth. It was very expensive. All natural fabrics and superbly tailored."

Kinsolving pulled the trigger. The laserifle hummed but the coherent bolt from its muzzle did not slay Cameron. The charge had drained through Kinsolving's repeated usage. The heat from the beam charred the front of the jacket and caused Cameron more pain—but it did not kill.

Kinsolving went berserk. He charged, swinging his laser like a club. Even with the adrenaline-powered attack, he was no match for Cameron. The trained killer stood silently, waiting, judging, then acting with blinding speed.

He batted away the laserifle barrel, stepped inside the circle of Kinsolving's arm and easily tossed him to the ground. Kinsolving landed with enough force to knock the wind from his lungs.

"So impetuous. You ought to know my training extends to fields other than robotics." Cameron reached down and grabbed Kinsolving's collar to pull him up.

"You will cease your conflict," came the curt command. A dozen Lorr, all with leveled weapons, moved to enforce that order.

A flash of disdain crossed Cameron's face. He said, "You lose, no matter what happens, Supervisor. I would have killed you. The Bizzies will lock you away on their prison world for the rest of your miserable life."

"Arrest him," shouted Kinsolving. "He's got the data on the plague that killed all the aliens on this world. It's in the computer block in his pocket."

"Wait," Cameron protested, hands raised. "He is a dangerous criminal. He killed one of your race."

"He is Barton Kinsolving, wanted for murder," agreed a Lorr policeman. "But we will also question you."

Cameron shot Kinsolving a look as hot as any laser beam. But Kinsolving felt no triumph. He had stopped Cameron and the data concerning the plague from returning to Gamma Tertius 4, but he had sacrificed himself in the process.

In winning, he had lost.

CHAPTER NINETEEN

BARTON KINSOLVING went cold inside when he saw the expression on Cameron's face. The sly grin made him wonder what vital point he had overlooked.

"In his pocket," Kinsolving said desperately. "A computer memory. It's got the data on the plague."

"You are a fugitive." The Lorr policeman stood impassively, his expression too alien for easy interpretation. Kinsolving saw, though, that he wasn't swaying the tall, limber-jointed alien.

"He's the murderer!" shouted Kinsolving. "He's responsible for the aliens dying on Paradise."

"Demented," Cameron said easily. "He ambushed me when I inspected property my company is considering for purchase."

"You can't let him go!"

"Both human ones," ordered the Lorr leader. The alien turned ninety degrees, his universal-jointed knee allowing the startling movement. He picked up his other foot, let his torso swivel to his intended direction of travel and stalked off.

Kinsolving and Cameron were both prodded along, but Cameron still showed no sign of uneasiness.

"They'll read the circuit and know," said Kinsolving. "You won't walk away, Cameron. They've got you."

"I won't be held. There is no formal charge lodged against me. Not on Paradise, not on any Bizarre world. You, though, are a desperate criminal fleeing your punishment. I did well informing the Lorr of your presence here."

"How did you know? Jessarette?"

"He showed me the photo taken aboard Almost Paradise. A clumsy man, Davi Jessarette," said Cameron. "A pity you had to kill him, too."

"You made sure I would. You said so!" Kinsolving tried to hold his anger in check. He knew Cameron was only goading him for the benefit of the Lorr. Kinsolving wondered which of the guards surrounding him carried a recorder taking down every word uttered. It could be any of them—or all.

He tried to determine logically what his best action might be. Cameron had found out about his presence on Paradise through Jessarette. He had alerted the Lorr. Had he done so anonymously? If he had put his name and legal likeness to the message summoning them, Kinsolving had no chance. The Lorr would think Cameron a fool for turning in one of his own kind, but publicly they would thank him.

And they would set the real killer free.

But Kinsolving doubted Cameron had signed the message personally. If any signature had been attached, it would be Jessarette's in his capacity as security officer for TR. The Lorr would be more prone to act on official notification.

"There, human things," said the Lorr officer. He shoved them into the flatbed of a cargo loader similar to the one Kinsolving had used earlier. "You will make no attempt to escape from my authority. Such crime will be instantly punished."

Kinsolving saw that the other Lorr watched attentively. He wondered what the price for failure would be if they let him escape again. Considering the size of the hunt they had already staged to find him, he thought it would be severe.

"I'll be glad to return to Gamma Tertius 4," said Cameron, lounging back. He favored his injured side where Kinsolving's laserifle bolt had burned him. Kinsolving had to sit upright, not even allowing his back to rest against the side of the bouncing loader. The pain that he had ignored for so long now welled up and threatened to overwhelm his senses. He had run too far, too fast, and been injured too many times.

All he wanted was to rest. But he dared not do that until he was sure that Cameron could not get the information back to Hamilton Fremont or any of the others on GT4.

"What do you get out of this?" Kinsolving asked. "A directorship?"

"Possibly," Cameron said, making a negligent gesture with his hand. "Such is of minor importance, compared to serving the Plan." He grinned. "There is so much activity concerning the Plan that one can overlook another important point. I am actually quite good at business matters. Intersellar Materials would profit from having me helping guide the entire corporation. After all, without the money-making capacity of the largest companies, the Plan would fall apart for lack of funding."

"Who is involved?" asked Kinsolving, intrigued in spite of himself. "I know IM's part. And Terra Recreations financed Suarez. What other companies?"

Cameron studied him, pale, cold eyes boring into Kinsolving's soul. "I rather think that is privileged information. I find it inconceivable that you will again escape the Lorr prison world. How you did that the first time I can only guess, but a finite risk exists that you might repeat this feat. It would be foolish of me to divulge more of the Plan to you."

"It's also crueler to let me imagine who is involved and what can happen."

"You have a good mind, Kinsolving. A pity you chose to betray your own kind in favor of . . . them."

Kinsolving smiled wickedly. "I'm not with them. Not in the way you think. I'm just trying to stay alive and do what's right. And you've made my life much easier."

"Oh?" Cameron raised a sandy eyebrow. "How have I done this?"

"The Lorr are cleverer at electronic spying than you are. Do you believe they'd stick us back here and not have surveillance? Everything you said about the Death Plan has been overheard. They know your part—and IM's."

"And," said Cameron, smiling in a way that chilled Kinsolving's enthusiasm, "you believe I have confessed and that you are going to be absolved of all crimes?"

The robotics genius shifted his weight slightly to one side and lifted his arm. A needle-thin one-centimeter-long robot clung to the fabric. Kinsolving saw a single red indicator light blinking on the machine like a baleful eye.

"What is it?"

"No," Cameron said, anticipating the man's question. "It isn't a jamming device. Rather, it is more sophisticated —and more subtle. The Lorr hear us speaking. The words, however, are supplied by my device. They might listen to their recording and, if they do, they will discover an innocuous little talk between us. I believe I programmed this one to substitute bantering dialog about sports. The Lorr would find it intensely boring, I am sure."

"Our voices wouldn't match. Voice ident would—"

"I'm sorry to crush your hopes. Voice identification *would* match. The robot records your words and then places them into my programmed patterns. A human expert could detect the differences. If they bothered to match our lips with our words, even the Lorr would see the difference."

"But they won't," Kinsolving said bitterly. The aliens did not expect confessions; they know who was guilty. Their courts had already decided. They would monitor only for disturbance or attempted escape.

"No," Cameron said softly, "they won't."

The cargo loader came to a smooth halt. The Lorr motioned for Kinsolving and Cameron to exit. Kinsolving frowned when he saw the building at the edge of the shuttle port. Paradise had no prison. Few criminals came here to ply their trade and with the constant surveillance, even the highest echelons of thieves would find the pickings difficult and sparse. But if Paradise had no formal prison, this building came close to providing an informal one. No windows had been cut into the thick plastic walls. Inside, Kinsolving saw little to give him hope. The original purpose for the small cubicles had long since been obscured by the addition of heavy mechanical locking bolts on the doors.

Kinsolving's only pleasure was fleeting. Cameron's face showed sudden concern. Anything electronic he could circumvent. Purely mechanical locks would pose a larger problem for him. But Kinsolving saw Cameron relax. The assassin had little reason to believe the Lorr would hold him.

"By the way," Cameron said as a Lorr guard shoved Kinsolving down the long, featureless corridor, "he murdered a Terra Recreations vice president, too. I'm sure you will find physical evidence near where you arrested him."

"Silence, human one," snapped the Lorr officer. "All materials have been impounded. We care nothing for violation of your local laws. However, in the spirit of cooperation and friendship between our cultures, this evidence will be given to human security personnel when we no longer require it."

"Just trying to help," said Cameron.

"The computer memory!" shouted Kinsolving as the Lorr guard shoved him into a tiny room. "Get it from Cameron. Read it!"

Kinsolving threw out his hands to keep himself from smashing facefirst into the wall. He winced in pain and turned. The room had been stripped of all furniture. The high ceiling contained a glow panel to provide light but Kinsolving couldn't jump high enough to touch it. The door closed firmly, and its heavy locking bars slid into place. The walls muffled the impact as he pounded on them. Even his laserifle might take several blasts to cut through plastic this thick. The impact laser might stand a better chance. But he didn't have it, either.

He had nothing but time. Kinsolving sank down to the floor and drew up his knees to his chest, arms circling his legs. He rested his head on his knees and tried to think.

Escape did not appear possible, but he could not resign himself to returning to the prison world. Better to die than be exiled to that brutal world for the remainder of his life. Dying presented moral problems, though, that had nothing to do with suicide.

If he died who would oppose the Stellar Death Plan? His death would be easy; untold worlds filled with living, breathing, thinking beings would also die. Kinsolving found this so repugnant that he knew he could not simply give up. He would continue fighting until the Plan was only a bad memory.

He looked up when the bolts securing the door pulled back. The Lorr officer and two others entered. In the corridor he saw three more aliens. He had no chance to overpower them and run.

"You, Barton Kinsolving. You will answer questions. How did you escape our prison world?"

"What about Cameron? Did you read out the computer memory block he had? It details how the plague virus was engineered. He intends to release the plague on thousands of your worlds."

"Mrs. Cameron has been cleared of charges in aiding

and abetting you. Evidence shows that he was another of your victims."

"He planned it all. He had Jessarette try to kill me. He set Denho against me."

"Mr. Cameron will be released."

"The computer block!" Kinsolving shouted. "At least study it. You've got nothing to lose and everything to gain."

Kinsolving dared to hope when he saw the expression on the Lorr's face. He had dealt with them often enough on Deepdig to know something of their thought processes. He had touched on a point the alien understood.

"The matter will be pursued further," the Lorr said. "How did you escape our prison world?"

"I did not kill your agent-captain on Deepdig," Kinsolving said, ignoring the Lorr's pointed question. "Cameron did. Check it. He was on-planet at the same time. He had been sent for that purpose by our superiors on Gamma Tertius 4."

"This is a matter beyond my jurisdiction. The court has decided your guilt. How did you escape the prison world?"

"You wouldn't commute the sentence if I told you?"

"Commute?" The officer turned and exchanged quick words in his own language with another Lorr. "I do not understand this word. How can a prison term be transported?"

"Never mind," said Kinsolving. The Lorr did not have the concept of leniency in their culture. He doubted that, even if they had, it would apply to a "human one."

The officer spoke rapidly with the others in the cell, then said to Kinsolving, "You will be taken away immediately upon clearance from this world. There is some difficulty in obtaining proper authorization due to your savagery."

"What?"

"It is believed that you had a part in the deaths of the planetary supervisor and the official in charge of this world. Further, evidence shows your involvement with the death of the security officer assigned by Terra Recreations to this world. Your crime wave has made our job more difficult."

"I . . ." Kinsolving bit off the words. He *had* killed Jessarette and Denho. Why deny killing Vandy and Suarez?

Two deaths, more or less, meant nothing to the Lorr. They had their fugitive and were content.

Spinning on their curiously jointed knees, they left the cubicle. The locking bars dropped back into place, turning this plastic room into a cell as secure as their prison world.

Kinsolving dropped his head once more to his knees, trying to think of some way out. If they searched Cameron, part of the Plan might be thwarted. And Fremont and Villalobos and the others on GT4 would not be pleased if Cameron lost the blueprint for manufacturing the bioweapon. This might place a strain on the cooperation between IM and TR. Anything that slowed the work of the Stellar Death Plan had to be good.

None of this helped Kinsolving. He dared not rely on Lark Versalles. She might not even know where the Lorr had taken him. Still, his thoughts kept turning to her. The *von Neumann* still hung in orbit. With luck, it had been repaired and was ready for departure.

Kinsolving caught his breath and held it. If the technicians had searched the cargo hold and found Rani duLong's body, it would only add to the charges against him. He hoped that Lark would have the sense to blame it all on him. An additional murder charge meant nothing to him.

The starship would be ready for flight. Kinsolving worked backward. Getting to Almost Paradise meant stowing away on the shuttle. Or perhaps not. Since Vandy's death, Paradise had to be in confusion. The Lorr had the evidence against him for killing Denho and Jessarette. The alien police officer might not have turned it over to what remained of the planetary security force.

So. He could shift away from this system if he got to the space station. He could get to Almost Paradise on the shuttle.

All Barton Kinsolving needed was a way to escape his cell.

"What would Cameron do?" he asked himself. "He's the master at this. Call down a robot and have it blast through the door?" Kinsolving shook his head at this fantasy. Even Cameron had seemed upset at the idea of being locked in a cubicle.

Something about Cameron chewed at the edges of Kinsolving's mind. Cameron had meticulously planned everything that had happened on Paradise. All the murders had been laid on Kinsolving's shoulders. The robot master knew Kinsolving would be returned to the Lorr prison world for the rest of his life.

"He wouldn't let a mere Bizzie take care of that," Kinsolving said aloud. "Cameron thinks they are incompetent. He holds them in deep contempt."

Even more telling was Cameron's ego. He would want the pleasure of killing Kinsolving himself for all the trouble he had been caused. Kinsolving had destroyed his part of the Plan on Zeta Orgo—and had injured him.

"Cameron wants me dead—and he would do it himself." Kinsolving tried different possibilities and always returned to this simple statement of Cameron's intentions.

"But how? A robot?" He looked around and saw no way for a robot to burrow in easily. And Cameron could not have known where the Lorr established their temporary headquarters. They had landed while he and Denho were fighting in the mansion and the woods beyond.

"He doesn't dare risk missing me when the Lorr load me into their ship. His robots are vulnerable to alien detection." Kinsolving remembered how the arachnoid policeman on Zeta Orgo 4 had easily destroyed Cameron's aerial assassins. Cameron never made the same mistake twice.

"He wants me dead. But how?"

Kinsolving mentally ran through every moment since confronting Cameron in the forest. He had tried to fire the laserifle; it had been almost drained; he had changed; Cameron easily threw him to the ground; Cameron lifted him by the collar and grinned. In triumph over—what?

Kinsolving reached back and ran his fingers along his collar. A tiny bead, cool and hard and small, sent a tingle all the way up his arm. Kinsolving skinned out of his tattered shirt and stared at the small device.

"Definitely Cameron's manufacture," he said softly. The device had no motile capability; he found no laser muzzle. "A bomb. What else can it be? Cameron has no need to spy on me. He wants me dead!"

Kinsolving bent closer and stared at the grain-of-rice-sized device. It could not hold much explosive, but at the back of his neck, it needed little to kill.

The tiny bomb shivered slightly. If Kinsolving had not been looking at it intently he would never have noticed.

He spun around and shoved the bomb and his shirt against the outer wall. He had been right. Cameron had sent the arming signal.

The bomb exploded with enough force to blow him backward across the cubicle.

But Kinsolving shouted in triumph. The bomb had blown a small hole through the thick outer wall of the cubicle. And the plastic had begun to burn with an ever-increasing ferocity. In seconds, a hole large enough for him to get through had been burned.

Barton Kinsolving held up the pieces of his shirt to shield his face from the heat, ran forward, tumbled through the wall and onto the tarmac. He had escaped!

CHAPTER TWENTY

BARTON KINSOLVING put his hands under his arms in an attempt to keep the oxygen off the burns. He looked over his shoulder and saw the ever-widening hole being burned in the plastic building wall. Whatever explosive Cameron had put into the small bomb had an incendiary effect not easily quenched.

Kinsolving ran on, almost stumbling, wanting to get out of sight. The Lorr would find out about his escape too soon. His muddled brain worked over the plan he had formulated.

"The shuttle," he muttered. "Up to the space station. To the yacht. Then shift to wherever the navigation computer locks onto first."

Weakness came over him in a debilitating wave. He stumbled and fell, rolled and came to his knees. Kinsolving looked up with bleary eyes and saw only a solid body. His eyes rose. For an instant he did not recognize her.

"The cosmetic dyes. You've reactivated them," he said to Lark.

"Barton!"

He fell forward, his pain too great to bear any longer.

When he awoke, he heard heavy equipment in the distance. One eye popped open and he cautiously studied his surroundings. Kinsolving feared that the Lorr had again captured him. But this did not seem a likely place to hold a dangerous escapee.

"Lark?"

"Here, Bart, darling," she said. The blonde slipped down beside the pneumatic-cushioned bed. She took his hand and held it gently. "I brought you back to the place Sheeda and I had stayed."

"The noises?"

Lark smiled wanly. "The robots have started renovating it for the next guests."

Kinsolving stretched. Little pain tore at his senses. Lark answered his unspoken question. "The automedic worked on you again. I had to destroy it because it wanted to put you into a life-coma. It said your wounds were very dangerous."

"I got away from Lorr," he said. "But I don't know whether I convinced them that Cameron had the computer memory block."

"I . . . Barton," she said almost contritely, "I didn't tell the Lorr about the plague."

"Why not?" Kinsolving knew he should be shocked or surprised or show some emotion. All that had drained from him. He floated softly, warm and content and beyond reaction.

"I didn't know how to do it. I had so much else to do. Sheeda." Lark swallowed hard. "Her remains are on the way back to Onar."

"I'm sorry," he said, meaning it.

"What would I say to the Lorr? Here, I happened to find a way of killing off your entire race?"

"Tell the Lorr that you stole it from Cameron." Kinsolving lay back, trying to drift off into unconsciousness and failing. "I've got to lift off-planet soon. We have to shift away from Paradise. There's nothing more for us to do here."

"Us, Bart?"

He turned and peered at her. Kinsolving knew how selfish it was of him to involve Lark. Her entire world revolved around parties, flitting from planet to planet and experiencing the life that the superrich enjoyed. Paradise was her sort of world. For him it carried more than a hint of decadence.

"I want to get Rani's body back to her brother. That's bothered me more and more. He deserves to know what happened to her."

Kinsolving closed his eyes and experienced a flash of guilt. How he misjudged her. Outwardly Lark was nothing more than a hedonistic rich kid. Now and again he saw traces of a real person beneath the surface.

"Get me up to Almost Paradise and I can get away. You can return to Earth with Rani's body. I don't think they've found it in the cargo hold. We would have been detained a long time ago if they had."

"I'll give the block circuit to the Lorr," she said, "but I can't promise any more." She dropped down, lying partially on him, and buried her face in his shoulder. He felt her shaking, and hot, wet tears soaked into his shirt. "I'm sorry, Barton. None of this is the way I want it. I get so confused. Why did Sheeda have to die? And Rani? And all the others?"

He said nothing. If it had not been for the Plan and trained killers such as Cameron and Jessarette, Lark's friends would still be alive.

Lark pushed away suddenly, tears making odd markings on her cheeks above the ever-changing flow of cosmetic dyes. The somber colors of the dyes told him that she was depressed.

"I'll do it now. You try to get aboard the same shuttle. We can create a diversion and the Lorr won't notice."

Kinsolving did not press the point. Such a scheme sounded too implausible to work, yet he had escaped from even worse situations. He heaved himself to a sitting position, let the dizziness pass, then stood. On legs that wobbled only slightly, he ordered fresh clothing from a robot servant, dressed, then he followed Lark from the room. The cab they took to the shuttle port was almost a relief. He had walked too much, with too many injuries, on Paradise.

"The Lorr," he said, pointing their guard positions out to Lark.

"Get down. When I go to them, slip into the departure room. There won't be much chance for you to get into the shuttle, so move fast."

He nodded. Lark stared at him, her eyes so blue that he felt a lump form in his throat. She bent and kissed him lightly, pressed one of her credit identicards into his hand, then jumped from the cab.

He started to call her back, to tell her to go directly to the departure areas and forget this, but it was too late. She walked briskly to the nearest Lorr and began talking animatedly with the alien.

Kinsolving slid from the cab and, bent low, hurried into

the departure lobby. The Lorr guarded the outside only; none were inside.

Still, Kinsolving dived for cover when he saw Cameron talking with a tall, well-built man in a dark blue business suit. From under the chair, Kinsolving peered up at the pair. He almost shouted when he saw Cameron reach into his pocket and pull out the computer block circuit and hand it to the man. It vanished into an inner pocket with the speed of light.

The pair went on talking, only a few words drifting to Kinsolving.

". . . go somewhere else before returning to GT4," Cameron said.

The other man nodded.

Both turned and faced the door when three Lorr entered. Kinsolving recognized the alien in the lead as the officer in charge.

"You, human one," the Lorr said, pointing at Cameron. "You will accompany us. There are serious charges filed against you."

"What charges can there be, sir?" asked Cameron. "This is a human-controlled resort, not a Lorr world. What crimes against the Lorr can I possibly commit?"

"We have examined the primitive computer memory circuits. The bioweapon released on this world that killed several of our citizens is detailed. You will endure questioning."

"Endure, yes," Cameron said, sighing. "I have no computer memory block and am quite innocent of these charges. I can prove it."

"There is a witness. She, too, is being detained."

Kinsolving heard this and stifled a curse. He had worried that Lark would be held as a witness, but there seemed to be no other way to stop Cameron other than direct confrontation.

And the Lorr ignored the man who had received the computer memory block from Cameron. They escorted Cameron away. The assassin never looked back or gave any hint that he had ever seen the courier before.

"Board for Almost Paradise," came the announcement.

Kinsolving scuttled from under the chair and ran to the

gate, sliding through just as it began to cycle shut. Four others besides the courier were on the shuttle. Kinsolving dropped into a vacant couch and let the acceleration press him down while he thought.

Aboard the shuttle was the wrong place to accost the courier and steal the block circuit. Aboard Almost Paradise presented problems, too. As on Paradise, surveillance was almost total. The only chance he held out was for him to steal the block memory just before the man boarded his ship for wherever he had decided to run.

It all worked out nicely. Kinsolving would steal it, the man would be on his way and unable to return, he would get aboard the *von Neumann* and wait for Lark, then they would leave. For Earth, for the edge of the universe, he just did not care any longer. He would succeed in destroying the block and keeping IM from distributing the virus.

With any luck, the Lorr would alert other worlds and doubly insure against the virus being used successfully.

The shuttle docked lightly and the other passengers left. The courier hung back. Kinsolving fumbled around, as if he had brought aboard luggage and could not get it freed from the small storage bins. He managed to out-fumble the courier. The man eventually left. Kinsolving followed closely.

All Kinsolving's careful plans vanished when he saw who awaited the courier.

"Ala," Kinsolving said softly, a catch in his voice. The woman he had loved, the woman who had betrayed him, caught up the courier in her arms and kissed him.

Kinsolving heard her say, "The ship is leaving in a couple minutes. You barely made it, Folle."

"I wouldn't miss it. Not if you were on it. Why, I'd have to swim through space to catch up!"

"Oh, Folle!" Ala Markken took the man's arm and the pair hurried along the corridor to a radial arm leading to the outbound ships.

Kinsolving stood and fought battles within himself. Ala and this man, Folle, boarded a ship going—where? He didn't know. But Folle had the block circuit that might destroy a thousand worlds. Even if the Lorr found a counter to the virus, a quick release might still kill billions.

He had to stop Folle. He had to destroy the block circuit the man carried.

And Ala!

Kinsolving ran after them. He ran to the airlock just as it began cycling shut. "Wait!" he called. "I'm supposed to be on the ship!"

A moment passed. The cycling machinery halted and a human operator appeared.

"Sir? I'm sorry. I missed your name on the passenger list."

"Where is this ship going?" demanded Kinsolving.

"To Hypon, sir."

"This is the one I want," he said firmly. Kinsolving saw the fleeting expression of disgust cross the man's face. It quickly melted into a smile when Kinsolving flashed the credit identicard that Lark had given him. The man took it and pressed it to an Accept panel.

"Very good, sir. Your credit has been approved for the flight. One minute while we open the locks. There. Have a good flight."

"Thank you for your courtesy. I know it's hard dealing with subphotonic space brains like me." Kinsolving made a self-deprecating gesture. The lock operator made no effort to contradict him.

Kinsolving sagged against the cool inner wall of the starship as the airlock cycled shut for the final time. Vibration from deep within the mighty ship grew. It prepared to shift away from Paradise and to the planet Hypon.

Barton Kinsolving stared at the blank wall and thought of Lark Versalles. He knew she would be all right. The Lorr would question her. He had no illusion about the Lorr charging Cameron with any crime. The man had been too clever by far. He had maneuvered Kinsolving into doing most of the killing; Vandy Azmotega's murder had been committed by Davi Jessarette. Cameron would return to Gamma Tertius 4 and await his courier, then turn over the deadly process for designing and incubating the virus to Fremont for use.

Kinsolving's ony hope lie in stopping the courier. Folle, Ala Markken had called him.

There would be time on the flight to steal the computer

memory circuit. And there would be time for him to determine whether Ala Markken had betrayed him intentionally.

Barton Kinsolving went to find an acceleration couch. This journey might prove a long one.

MASTERS OF SPACE

**The new action-packed
SF adventure series
in the pulse-pounding tradition of
E.E. "Doc" Smith**

Robert E. Vardeman

**THE STELLAR
DEATH PLAN**   75004-x/$3.50US/$4.95Can

One man stands alone against a deadly intergalactic conspiracy.

THE ALIEN WEB   75005-8/$2.95US/$3.95Can

Hunted through the galaxy, Kinsolving must prevent a horrifying secret scheme for planetary genocide.

**A PLAGUE
IN PARADISE**   75006-6/$2.95US/$3.95Can

On the planet Paradise, Kinsolving uncovers a deadly new biological weapon—a DNA unraveling virus.

Buy these books at your local bookstore or use this coupon for ordering:

AVON BOOK MAILING SERVICE, P.O. Box 690, Rockville Centre, NY 11571
Please send me the book(s) I have checked above. I am enclosing $_____
(please add $1.00 to cover postage and handling for each book ordered to a maximum of three dollars). *Send check or money order*—no cash or C.O.D.'s please. Prices and numbers are subject to change without notice. Please allow six to eight weeks for delivery.

Name _____

Address _____

City _____ State/Zip _____

MOS 9/87